RARE FORM

DESCENDED OF DRAGONS
BOOK I

BY
JEN CRANE

Published by Carpe Noctem Publishing LLC
Edited by Lacey Thacker
Cover Design by Deranged Doctor Designs

Rare Form
All Rights Are Reserved. Copyright 2015 by Jen Crane

First electronic publication: October 2015
First print publication: October 2015

Digital ISBN: 978-0-9965756-0-7
Print ISBN: 978-0-9965756-1-4

To Suzy
for sowing the seed.

To Brock
for sunlight, nourishment, and roots.

To colleagues BB, KG, LC, MM and LT
for encouraged growth and selective pruning.

Also by Jen Crane

DESCENDED OF DRAGONS SERIES
Origin Exposed
Betrayal Foretold

www.JenCraneBooks.com

For news and releases: http://bit.ly/Jen_Crane_Newsletter

I left the science building when my nine-thirty astronomy class dismissed and tossed my backpack into the passenger seat. The Beast, a not-quite-fully-refurbished but much-loved '67 Mustang, purred to life. It didn't have power steering or air, but it had style.

The thin black steering wheel groaned under the pressure of my grip as my thoughts turned to an impending college graduation, a lack of plans for the future, and the absence of a career path. You'd think all of that would be settled, but…nope. I was soon to receive a degree for which I had no real-life application from a university for which I felt no real connection. Because going to college was what was expected after high school.

I adjusted my sunglasses in response to the brightening May horizon and chewed my lip as I began obsessing, again, about the twenty-thousand in student debt I'd racked up thanks to the exorbitant and ever-increasing cost of a degree.

Wham!

Thoughts of joining the real world evaporated.

Time suspended, and the scene before me played out in slow motion. In the span of two heartbeats my world became devoid of sound, of rational thought—there was only reaction

1

as a sharp, jarring impact snapped my head to the side and catapulted the car into oncoming traffic.

My beloved Mustang was not only spinning in a circle, but toppling side over side. As the car thrust down, flipped over, and crashed roughly again onto the pavement I grabbed at handles, braced my legs, and scrabbled for purchase of any solid surface to prevent being tossed around the car like a pinball.

It seemed an eternity before the Mustang bounced a final time and stuttered to a stop. I let out the breath I'd been holding and looked around aimlessly, confused. Air rushed back into my lungs that smelled of burning rubber and the bitter, complex odor of overheated electronics.

Out. I needed to get out of the car. But I wasn't sitting upright. The left side of my body leaned heavily against the driver's side door. The only thing visible through the windshield was a bent-up cherry red hood. A shock of pain that weakened my knees shot through my neck as I sought out the skyward-facing passenger door. I ground my teeth, put a hand to my neck, and made an effort not to move so suddenly again.

Unbuckling my seatbelt with one hand, I shimmied around inside the car to kneel upright. The car's interior was out of proportion and the passenger door had been badly damaged. The door handle above taunted me, guarding the only way out. I pushed the passenger door with all of my strength, but it was so jammed it wouldn't budge. Short, panicked breaths didn't provide enough oxygen for my addled brain to function properly, and I kicked and punched at everything in futile effort. I was stuck.

And something was definitely burning.

The car's interior provided no avenue of escape, hard as I tried. But my search was derailed when the pace of my panicked heart skyrocketed. My chest burned painfully and I rubbed at it to find relief. None came. My heart felt full, hard—like a grossly over-inflated ball . It beat hard— Kathump, Kathump—and flopped over inside my chest as an overwhelming sense of dread nearly drowned me before settling in the pit of my stomach.

Was this a panic attack? Of course it was. They'd been happening more frequently lately.

With a hand to the back of my throbbing neck I searched the disheveled car for something to break a window, but my belongings had been strewn wildly from the roll. I dug around the console and finally found a metal flashlight. Just as I reached back to swing at the window, the passenger door gave a grating creak and opened half way.

A thick mop of black hair came into view as a low, rough voice urged, "Give me your hands. I'll pull you up."

Thankful for the help, I did as instructed and was swiftly pulled from the smoking car.

Before I could form a word of thanks, my rescuer threw me over his shoulder and shot across the road. As he ran my head beat against his back, which exacerbated my neck pain, and I closed my eyes in misery.

At first I was too shocked to protest. Everything had happened so fast. Wreck. Roll. Fire. Escape. Manhandled? Besides what I suspected to be whiplash, I wasn't seriously injured. I took a quick inventory. A little pain, but overall surprisingly intact. Everything seemed to be in working order. So why was I being carried? My feminine sensibilities were offended and I wanted down.

"Hey," I hollered. "Put me down. I'm okay. I can walk."

Nothing.

I tried to raise up, but a big hand at the small of my back forced me back down. "Ugh. Stop for a minute and put me down," I pleaded. "Please."

Still he ran.

For the first time I made note of who was carrying me, or at least I took stock of the limited view I had. Despite hanging upside down halfway down his body, I was still quite high above the ground. He was tall. And strong. He jogged as if I weighed nothing at all. An off-duty fireman? No. His dark pants looked expensive, as did black dress shoes. My face bounced against a crisp white dress shirt that was still tucked in.

I growled in frustration as I kicked my legs and slapped at his sides. "Put. Me. Down."

My auburn hair flew wildly back over my head when he stopped without a word and set me down against a tree. I let out a grunt of irritation before glancing at his retreating form and taking took a good look at my surroundings. He'd deposited me in a mulched flowerbed fifty yards from my car. I turned too sharply toward it and groaned when another shot of pain speared through my neck.

Intent on getting back to the scene of the accident I stood and dusted the seat of my jeans and noticed my shoulder was stiff, too.

But pain would have to wait. My car was the primary concern, and I held my breath as I searched for it. The Earth itself froze on its axis when I spotted it smashed against a light pole at the four-way intersection. My beloved car lay beaten, battered, and unrecognizable. It would never be the same.

Just as I got my dobber in the dirt...whoof, the back underside of the Mustang burst into flames. I choked and coughed on a breath sucked in too fast as flames engulfed the entire car.

"Oh, god, no." I stumbled back, my hands flying to my head in despair. This reaction hurt both my neck and my shoulder and I groaned pitifully.

My instinct was to run to the car—to save it. I started for it but the Good Samaritan grabbed me just above the elbow and held me there, looking on, until I realized the stupidity of that course of action.

The day old lady Benson sold The Beast to me was one of my luckiest. It sat in a hay barn for years after Mr. Benson died. When I was sixteen, after years of saving baby- and dog-sitting funds, I found the nerve to ask if she would sell it. She'd already told everyone in the county no. I don't know what got into her that day, but she looked me over with a cloudy eye and croaked "All right. I'll take twenty-five hundred and not a penny less." It was a steal, and left me plenty to get it up and running.

Most of the girls at school had cute little sedans or the occasional SUV, but I loved my Mustang. I would normally have bought something that got great gas mileage, saver of the planet that I was, but I was doing my part by re-using the old Mustang, right?

The loss of my car and the shock of the accident were too much. My lip quivered uncontrollably before grief swallowed me whole. Big, hot tears streamed down my cheeks. I wiped my splotched face on my sleeve and thought, Oh, you really are a loser now, Stonewall. No job, no car, and no prospects for either. This I found wildly hilarious and laughed as hard as I'd cried. A new kind of tears formed and fell.

"Sit back down; you're in shock," ordered that same deep voice.

His words sunk in and I thought he must be right. Laughing hysterically was not an appropriate response to a near-death car wreck and ensuing pyrotechnic display.

"Your forehead's bleeding," he said. "And you're going to have quite a bump. Maybe a concussion and whiplash, too. Sit back down. Let me see if you're injured anywhere else."

I sunk to the hard ground in a daze. As he busied himself examining me I sat cross-legged and watched in horror as my beloved car suffered a slow, smoldering death.

A huge black Range Rover sat nearby, its front end smashed. That's the bastard that hit me, I thought. Where's the driver? There were too many people wandering around to determine the owner. I glanced around wildly, but closed my eyes on a shaky exhale when pain shot through my neck and back.

When the spasms died down I opened my eyes to find Super Helpful Samaritan sitting on his heels looking at me. Hard. His attention demanded reciprocation, and when I finally saw him I lost my breath in a rush. I'd never seen a man like him in my life. He was older than I'd ever go for, but holy bejesus he was spectacular.

The mess of black hair I first caught a glimpse of in my car was longer on top than the closer-cropped sides and fell recklessly around his head. Amber-colored eyes bored into mine. His eyes were absolutely breathtaking; the color of aged whiskey and framed by dense black eyelashes. They were searching for something—probing—and seeing too much. I wanted a jacket, some way to cover up and hide. I forced myself to look away.

After a moment of feigning interest in a speck on my jeans, I peeked back to see he'd moved on, too. He squeezed and bent various joints—I assumed to ensure nothing was broken. Big thumbs rolled along my neck and into my hairline, applying slight pressure. Everywhere he touched felt warm, overcharged, tingly. Having a stranger's hands probe me in such an intimate way should have horrified or repulsed me, but repulsion was the last thing I felt.

Still intent on his work, he crooked a finger under my chin and lifted my face. He pushed a mess of my hair back from my forehead as he dabbed at the side of my face with...

"What is that?"

"Part of my shirt," he said. "Hold still."

"So bossy," I grumbled. I waited, if a little impatiently, until he finished.

"Well, you've mostly stopped bleeding and that's good." He pulled the scrap of shirt away from my head and I saw that it was caked in blood. "You'll be sore for a few days from the impact. No signs of concussion, and the neck pain should be fading." His gaze shot down to my chest and I swear I caught the faintest hint of a grin before he resumed his clinical assessment. "You'll have a nasty seatbelt burn, but that'll heal in time, too."

I looked down and noticed, for the first time, that my shirt was badly askew and I had a raw red mark from the top of my left breast across my shoulder. Lovely. I rearranged my shirt and pretended to have some semblance of dignity left.

He cleared his throat to hide another grin, but he wasn't fooling anyone—especially me—though I chose to ignore him.

I rolled my shoulders and stretched my neck from side to side. Oddly, I already felt better. Not so much pain as before.

"Thanks for getting me out of the car," I said. "And thanks for the medical attention. I'm Stella Stonewall."

His wide mouth opened and closed two or three times before he finally permitted it to form a genuine smile. His eyes gleamed with pleasure and he shook his head, his eyebrows stretching toward his hairline in disbelief. Then he laughed. Full-on, mouth-open, head-thrown-back laughed.

He. Was. Beautiful.

"What's so damned funny?" He was a hottie and all, but a righteous headache had me feeling prickly. My favorite thing in the whole world had just blown up as I watched. Definitely not my favorite day.

He quirked a brow at my biting tone, then shook his head good-naturedly again.

"Listen," I said. "I'm just not having a great day, ok? I loved that car. I'm gonna kill the sonofabitch who hit me. And yes, I tend to curse. A lot, when I'm pissed. Excuse the hell outta me."

I smirked, but immediately felt childish for the unnecessary expletives.

"What's so funny," he said, ignoring my outburst, "is that my day has taken a serendipitous turn for the better. I came to this town in search of a girl, and she ran right into me. Literally. I've been looking for you, Stella Stonewall." It was his turn to smirk.

My stomach churned with confusion and unease. Why was this guy looking for me? Although he was…beyond handsome, my whole body felt like a tuning fork. My scalp prickled and my internal weirdar blinked Warning. Warning. Danger. Danger.

I squinted because the more I looked—really looked—at him, the more I saw there was something not quite normal about him. He seemed…I don't know…different. I took in his size and the fact that he had effectively carried me out of anyone's earshot and eyesight, and that panicky feeling came back.

I shot to my feet and inched toward the accident—and the crowd. "I'd better go talk to the guy that hit me. The cops'll be here soon and I'll need to give a statement."

He held me by the arm, a vice on my bicep.

"You ran that red light," he said and shook my arm just hard enough to scare me. "You didn't even slow down. You hit me. Hard."

"It was you?" I gasped in outrage. My spine infused with indignation, and I jerked my arm from his grasp. "The hell I ran a red light! I was just driving, minding my own business, when someone crashed into the side of me." Right? I was absorbed in my own thoughts as I drove and…I wasn't so sure anymore. Did I hit him?

"The reason I hit you," he said, "is because my light was green. You came speeding through the intersection in that steel contraption you were driving; you never even slowed. Actually, that car is probably the only reason you're still alive. They just don't make them like they used to." He sighed and shook his head wistfully.

"My beautiful Beast," I whispered, tears threatening to spill over as I was once again overwhelmed with emotion. "You saved my life, girl. Traded mine for your own."

He looked from the smoking mass to me and back again. He closed his eyes and let out a tired breath that clearly communicated 'Oh great. She's a psycho,' but changed the subject. "Don't worry about the authorities," he said. "I'll take care of that. But you're right. We'll need to go and sort this out. We can take care of our other business after that."

I didn't care to question him further about this 'other business.' Considering the scary vibes I was picking up, my goal was to get to the scene of the accident, find a phone, and have someone pick me up. ASAP.

The police had arrived and were questioning witnesses. Miraculously, no one seemed to have seen anything.

I tried to give my statement to an officer, but Señor Samaritan approached like he was the mayor. He loomed over me with a possessive bearing. He was too close, too much.

"Excuse me," I sidestepped him and shook my head in a "back-the-eff-off" gesture. "I'm trying to talk to Officer..." I checked the gold badge at the officer's chest, "Officer Polk."

"The officer has all he needs," my rescuer said. "There'll be no need for a report. We can leave as we like."

He said this as if it was the most sensible thing in the world. And he was so confident that I almost believed it myself. I would have, too, if not for those same bells going off in my head. Lucky I had such keen senses. My mother always chalked them up to a woman's intuition, but mine were overdeveloped. I knew a weirdo when I saw one.

"...no need for a report. You two are free to go," Officer Polk concluded. I squinted suspiciously at Hot Creepy Rescuer Guy and the officer walked away without another word leaving me alone, again, with...

"What's your name, anyway? My name seems to be of interest to you; I'd like to know yours." Damn, I forgot to use the officer's phone.

"Gresham. Rowan Gresham. I'm so glad to finally find you, Stella."

"What? Why?" I sputtered and took a step backward.

"We'll clear up everything in time. Shall we go? My Rover's still operational."

I shook my head determinedly. "No. That's okay. I'll call a friend."

I took a step toward the throng of people, but he went on as if I hadn't spoken. "I'll call a tow to deal with your car. I'm afraid both it and anything you had in it are gone. I'm sorry."

I hadn't yet thought of that. My laptop, my handbag, everything in my backpack was burned to a crisp. What a freakin' day. "Listen, mister," I said. "I appreciate the offer, but I don't know you and, frankly, you're creeping me out. There's no way I'm getting in a car with you. I'll go over to that coffee shop and borrow the phone."

9

"Get in the car, Stella," he grated. "We have a lot to discuss. I'm not going to hurt you. I'm only here to talk to you." He must have been losing his patience because I could see the muscles in his jaw contract as he gritted his teeth. My ears rang and I had the strangest sense he was trying to coerce me into the car.

"Huh-uh," I shook my head again. "Nope. What, you have some ice cream in there? Candy? Maybe some puppies you want to show me?"

That was it. I was determined not to waste any more time with him. The muscles in my legs jumped and tensed, anticipating my next move. With what I thought was lightening speed I lifted a leg to run for the coffee shop. But before my foot had even touched the ground, he'd thrown me back over his shoulder and headed for the Range Rover.

The force of it knocked the breath from my lungs and my eyes shot wildly around the landscape as I gasped for air. I could see everything in that moment. Traffic was backed up due to our accident. Several people milled around my car, pointing at the charred mass. Others went on about their day as if nothing had happened. I could see everything; why could no one see me?

I kicked and hit and screamed at my captor, my body rigid with fear the second time he manhandled me. This wasn't a rescue, but a kidnapping. He ignored my efforts, which did nothing to slow his clipped pace. Time wasn't on my side. I stilled for a moment and his grip loosened almost imperceptibly. Gathering both my physical and mental strength, I twisted my body to throw myself from his shoulder. It worked. I fell right into his arms. He looked down at me irritably as thick muscles jerked me into his chest.

Despite my frantic bucking and attempts to bite everything in close range, he managed to buckle me into the back seat of his Range Rover and slammed the door.

It wasn't my day for success with door handles. For all my efforts tugging and manipulating, the door was locked and there was no manual way to undo it. The pounding of my fists on the window competed with my ragged screams for help, but it was useless. No one heard me.

My circumstances had degraded fast, and the situation was serious— life-and-death serious. I needed a plan.

I searched my pockets and the back of the car for something to strangle him from behind, but came up empty handed. My only defense was to attack him. I considered doing it as he drove, but ruled that out. I'd hate to survive one wreck only to be killed in another.

My best option was to attack him when he opened the door to do god-knew-what with me. I had taken a self-defense class my sophomore year for a PE credit. What was that acronym? Oh yeah, S.I.N.G. for Solar-plexus, Instep, Nose, Groin.

My heart pounded furiously within my chest and I feared another panic attack. Sure, being kidnapped and thrown into a car with a strange man was reason to panic. But I considered myself a woman of action, one who in the face of fight or flight would always choose to fight. These panic attacks were useless and demoralizing. I was angered by them. Ashamed. Anytime anxiety or anger or stress approached, my heart raced and beat so hard within my chest that the vibrations racked my petite body.

Breathing deeply, I made an effort to calm down. Tried to mentally prepare myself to whip the guy's ass. Okay, at least to stun him long enough to escape. But then my thoughts turned to the loss of my beloved Beast, to being physically forced into a car…I was furious. I wanted to attack him, to hurt him.

Rowan Gresham cleared his throat in the front seat and looked at me through the rear view mirror. His expression was guarded, tense. "All right, Stella, we're at your apartment."

My guts heaved with dread at his words. The back of my neck broke out in a cold sweat and suddenly I was a rabbit in a snare.

What were we doing at my place? Shouldn't he be taking me to an underground bunker to keep me locked up and abused until he tired of me and found another? And how did he know where I lived? As if there weren't grounds enough already for me to be freaked-the-hell-out.

"I'm going to open your door," he said slowly. "Please, let's go inside peaceably. There's a lot I need to tell you. A lot you need to know. And we don't have much time."

"Mmm-hmm. Sure. Let's go in my apartment where no one can hear me scream," I muttered.

I steeled my nerves and held my breath as he opened the door. I could do it. I would kick him in the stomach, and then again in the face when he doubled over in pain. Then I would run for a neighbor.

Gresham opened the door and I kicked, hard, heel-first into his stomach. But he didn't fold in pain as I'd anticipated. Instead he grunted and managed to grab both of my hands and use them to pull me out of the car. I continued to kick whatever I came in contact with. He huffed in pain, pulled both of my arms behind my back and lifted straight up, forcing me to my knees.

"Ow-ow-ow. Let me go. Someone help me. Help!" I screamed, but no one came to my rescue.

I was pulled to my feet, my hands still held behind my back with just enough pressure to disable me as we crossed the lot toward my apartment. He opened the door, which had, to my extreme dismay, been left open by whoever last left. I yelped as he shoved me down onto the sofa before backing away.

His chest expanded with two or three deep breaths. "I'm not going to hurt you," he said. "Calm down and give me an opportunity to tell you why I'm here." This was delivered in a calm, soothing tone as if he was addressing a spooked horse. I imagine that's what I looked like. I certainly felt like an edgy mare. My hands shook with such force that clasping them together only forced the vibrations up to my teeth, which chattered in time to my racing pulse.

Gresham stood back from me, obviously afraid to make another move. With a great deal of effort, I switched tactics. I nodded my head slowly and forced a relaxed expression. My hands only slightly shook when I placed them on my knees and scooted toward the edge of the sofa.

"All right," I said. "I've calmed down."

Gresham's high cheekbones looked even more severe in his irritation, but he nonetheless stalked toward me. "Good, now, where to begi—Ooof."

I launched myself at him, intending to get a good shot at his eyeballs...or the other pair of balls...whatever I came in contact with. The move was naive, ill-advised. Just as I thought I was doing a fair job of attacking, he flipped me onto my back, straddled my hips, and held my hands above my head.

"Dammit, girl." His growl was laced with more than irritation. "Will you stop this? I just want to talk to you." He was furious. His breath came hard and his face was dark, severe. The bulk of him towered over me, and I couldn't see anything around his wide-set shoulders.

"Yeah? Tell that to your pants, asshole." I could feel his substantial erection pressing onto my pelvic bone as he sat atop me, looming over me and pinning down my arms as I fought to free myself. I should've known putting up a fight would turn on someone like him.

I wondered frantically where my roommate, Lizzie, was before the harsh reality of my circumstances set in. No one was going to save me. Fear and panic were replaced by despair, and my throat swelled and convulsed with emotion. Tears welled in my eyes as I met Gresham's gaze. Despite my nearly crippling fear, I swallowed past the lump in my throat, and with the full force of my gaze pleaded with him not to hurt me, to walk away.

Gresham's face fell in horror as realization dawned, and before a single tear could fall, he was off of me and across the room. The barstool scraped loudly over the aged linoleum as he drug it from its nest beneath the counter. He fell roughly onto the stool and buried his face in his hands.

For several moments neither of us dared breathe. The tone of his voice had changed when he spoke again. It was remorseful; almost tortured. "I'm sorry, Stella," he said.

"I...there's nothing I can say to excuse my behavior. But please try to forgive me. I assure you you were never in any danger. It's just a physical response. I have no desire to...I would never...I'm sorry."

The defeated set of his shoulders and the fear and panic in his eyes told me he was completely horrified. I believed him—at least in that.

"I can see no productive conversation can be had today," he said. "I'll leave. But I must speak with you, and soon. Will you meet me tomorrow morning?"

"What, so you can kidnap me again? I don't think so. Get the hell out of my house."

His face, until then contrite, flashed rage before he caught himself. "Stella, I have information on your father. And there is more I—"

My head jerked in confusion at the mention of my father. I'd never known him, and my mother was stubbornly silent on the topic. I had tried for years to find information about him. I didn't know the story of their courtship or my conception. As any child would, I asked why I didn't have a daddy like the other kids at school. Mom either changed the subject or told me families come in all shapes and sizes and we were lucky to have each other. When it's all you know, you accept your reality and move on. She never remarried; she never dated.

"My father?" I breathed. "What could you know of my father?"

"I know important things you don't," he said, his brow furrowing with the emotion behind his words. "And much that you should."

I worried my lip between my teeth; shook my head. Despite my attempt not to, the fact was I believed him. "I do want to know about my father," I said. "But I also want you out of this apartment." My head throbbed with the effort to form a plan. I wanted whatever information he claimed he had, but wasn't comfortable being alone with him. "I'll give you my number. You can call me later. After we've had a chance to calm down. You can tell me whatever's so important then."

His amber eyes took on a kinder look. A gentler one. "It's not that simple, I'm afraid."

"Why not?"

"It's…it's complicated. And incredible. Besides, there's something I'd like to show you."

"Yeah, I'll bet," I mumbled, and he shot me a censorious look.

"Look, do you want to learn about your father or not?" he asked. He had me at a disadvantage, and he knew it. I was desperate for information. When I made no answer he continued, "Let's meet somewhere public in the morning. Did you see the coffee shop near the accident today?"

We agreed to meet and he let himself out, wary of getting too close and frightening me again. The moment he was gone, I engaged both the handle and deadbolt locks, then headed down the hall to my room and shut the door.

I crashed face-first onto my fluffy down comforter and let the tears flow. I cried in release of the panic that had overwhelmed me over the last hour. I cried for my beloved car, and for my favorite handbag. I cried because I had no idea what to do next, and I cried because I always thought my life would turn out differently, that it would be epic. I cried because it was the third time I'd cried that day when I never got emotional. And I cried because my nose was running and my tissue box was empty. Next thing I knew, streaks of morning sunlight skimmed across my sleep-swollen face, warming my cheeks despite the cold dread I felt inside.

I had reason to be wary of Rowan Gresham when I saw him at the coffee shop. Crazy doesn't always look crazy. Sometimes it looks like the most handsome and refined gentleman ever encountered in one's short life.

Gresham sat at a corner table for two but the confident set of his shoulders, the rigid turn of his jaw, and the indiscriminate menace in his glare occupied the space of half a dozen. The pendant light above him had blown, providing a concealing shadow, and despite the prime coffee consumption hour the tables around him stood deserted. I wasn't the only one who picked up on his threatening vibe.

The gray counter near the register betrayed streaks of white from repeated abuse as half conscious and completely-apathetic baristas slid hot beverages across it day after day. I ordered a large latte and added a shot of mocha at the last minute because I sure deserved it after the day I'd had.

The air in the coffee shop was infused with the thick, robust aroma of coffee beans, and I took a fortifying breath. Blind courage was what I needed to face him again. It had gotten me this far. Just a bit further yet to go.

I made my way to the back table and sat across from Gresham, who stood while I approached and sat again once I was seated. This unfamiliar display of chivalry pleased me, but I hastily remembered I hated him and quelled any gushy feelings.

"Thank you for coming, Stella. I had my doubts you would. Do you care for anything besides coffee?"

Rowan Gresham had a slight accent. Not English, exactly. Not French. I couldn't quite place it, but it seemed to have the influence of a romance language. He rolled the "r" in 'care.' Sexy.

No, Stonewall. He's a weirdo, remember?

His lightweight black sweater probably cost more than my entire ensemble, which that day was nothing to sneeze at. I'd worn my navy sheath dress, the one cut a little too low in the back and a little too high in the hemline. A patterned belt cinched my waist and defined the line of my chest. Casual ballet flats ensured the outfit still said 'daytime.'

"I almost didn't." I forced the words out and raised my chin. "But I couldn't overcome my curiosity." Nerves inspired me to swipe an imaginary strand of auburn hair behind my ear. "So? Let's hear it. What do you know about my father? And just so you know," I warned, "I asked the woman at the counter to keep an eye on our table, should you get any more ideas about throwing me over your shoulder. And three people know I'm meeting you." A complete lie. I hadn't even told my roommate Lizzie the truth about the meeting.

"Yes, I'm sorry about that," he stammered uncomfortably. "But you must admit that the first time was to save your life, and the second…well, I did need you to get you into the car quickly." To his credit, he looked abashed as his gaze shot to the floor and he licked dry lips.

"Well, let's get right down to it, then, Mr. Gresham." I sat back in my seat, crossed my arms and gave him my best scowl—eyebrows pulled together in the middle and everything. "What do you want to tell me so desperately that you were willing to kidnap me?"

He gave me a smile that was less like a smile and more like a you-were-cute-for-a-minute-but-now-shut-the-hell-up.

"I have some information I'm afraid is going to give you a bit of a shock. There's no real way to ease into it. The world…you…things are not what they seem."

He was silent for a moment and scrunched up his face, turning his head from side to side as if he was trying to work out some great mystery. He hesitated so long I thought he wouldn't go on. But then he set his square jaw and nodded once.

"Look, I'll just dive right into it. Stop me if you have questions. There exists a whole other realm in which beings have varying lineages, abilities, knowledge. This world is parallel to the one you know, but it is vastly different. My world knows of yours, of course, but very few people within your world have the slightest idea about mine."

"Well, sure," I said and leaned back in my chair to look over my shoulder and see if a) anyone had overheard the whackjob, and b) I could make it to the exit before he grabbed me again.

"You will undoubtedly find this impossible to believe, and for that reason and for the sake of saving valuable time, I've brought a substantial token of proof of my world's existence."

I was reeling from his sudden louie into Looney Land, but this profession did grab my attention. Visions of tin-foil Fedoras and Hot Pockets bearing the likeness of Baby Jesus filled my mind as I waited for him to produce his 'proof.'

Idly, I concluded it was surely one of life's great travesties that such a fine specimen of a man was a raging nut-job.

I looked up to find Gresham glancing nervously around the coffee shop. He put his hands under the table and motioned with his head and eyes that I should look down.

I rolled my eyes. "Oh, great. More penis tricks. No freakin' way." I shook my head on a smirk. The guy was unbelievable.

His eyes bulged and his jaws clenched in silent disapproval of my resistance. He made a jerky nod toward the floor again.

"Oh, what the hell. Seen one, you've seen 'em all." I leaned over and peeked at what he wanted so badly to show me under the table.

What I saw under that table shelved any further sarcasm because there, plain as the smirk on my face, was the tiniest person I had ever seen. Dressed in a three-piece brown tweed suit, he looked more like an old-world attorney than a mythical creature, though he did have facial hair enough to deserve the gnome moniker. Or was that a gnomiker? The distinguished little man stood with hands on his hips and tapped a foot in impatience. Despite being the size of a large doll, he managed to look down his spectacles at me and raised a furry eyebrow in the universally understood, 'Well, seen enough?'

I nodded numbly in answer to his silent question. Gresham offered his own nod of thanks to the little man, and then he was gone.

I aimed for cool and collected, but my heart raced madly and my mouth was so dry I couldn't move my tongue. I reached for my latte, but my hand shook so that I returned it to my lap. I smoothed my dress against my legs in an attempt to rid my hands of their sudden moisture.

No. I did not just see what I thought I saw. Not possible.

"Since you seem to be at a loss for words—a phenomenon I don't take lightly since in my experience you rarely have little to say—I'll proceed."

I shook my head dumbly—again—so Gresham continued.

"My world is made of beings far different than this one. The major variant between the two is that humans on Earth evolved from primates, while the residents of Thayer evolved from many groups within the animal kingdom. Thayerians trace their ancestry from hoofed animals like deer and horses, from wolves, bears, amphibians, as well as primates."

My eyes lost focus as I considered his words.

"Are you still with me?"

"Yes," I croaked. My brain-to-mouth function was firing at a snail's pace.

"Another marked difference is that Thayer is a far more magical realm. Since it's much older, and our people have varying lineages and talents, we have developed and learned to control supernatural abilities."

19

I didn't believe what he was saying for one minute. *Another world?* No. I'd know if something, somewhere else existed. *Wouldn't I?* Astrophysicists and astronomers would know if worlds existed parallel to ours. *Wouldn't they?*

"You expect me to believe all this? That there's another world out there where people evolved from wolves and birds?"

"I know it will be hard to accept," he said.

"You have got to be kidding me," I scoffed. "You're trying to demolish the foundation of the very existence I've stood on my entire life, and you think it'll be 'hard to accept'?"

"I'm sorry, Stella. This situation is unusual. I'm doing the best I can. Please try to keep an open mind."

"Having an open mind would mean trying bok choy or bungee jumping. What you're asking is outrageous, Mr. Gresham. A parallel world? Come on."

He didn't address my protests, but continued, "Ironically, despite having been in existence far longer than this one, ours is a world that exists now as yours once did—an age gone by, a simpler way of life, but with the benefit of modern technology and scientific knowledge. It is a world that I wish yours had turned out to be. But somewhere along the line people of your developed world began seeking fortunes and possessions forgot what the pursuit of happiness is all about."

I was not offended at Gresham's negative synopsis of our culture. It was true, after all, especially in first world countries. As I pictured the world he described and imagined simpler times and hairier people, I found that his description of this 'alternate realm' sounded dreamy. I mean, I loved an episode of Andy Griffith as much as the next girl. Throw in magic and technology and, well, sold.

Sadly, his description of a variegated utopia made it obvious that poor Mr. Gresham's elevator did not go all the way to the top floor. Bless his heart, he was an egg roll short of a pu pu platter.

On the other hand I had just seen a real-life gnome. Perhaps I was the one *thisclose* to converting to Scientology.

"All right," I said. "Let's say—hypothetically—your perfect little magic world does exist, and I really did just see with my own eyes a tiny little professor. Why did you hunt me down? Why tell me all this? What does it have to do with me? And what can you tell me about my father?"

"Yes, well..." The sides of Gresham's mouth pulled back and down to reveal a thin line of his bottom teeth. "This is the difficult part, isn't it?" He shrugged and let out a long breath. "One of your parents was born in our world. You're half Thayerian. And despite being only partially so, you already have or will inherit certain....abilities...characteristic of your family's lineage."

I sat, mouth agape, for what seemed like an eternity. I ran his last statement over and over in my head, denying its possibility outright. For fun I tried to imagine my mother as an otherworldly being. I mean, she ain't right, but I would never have considered her 'alien.'

I wasn't ready to board Gresham's locomotive to Locotown and shook my head in an effort to clear it. What he said could not be true. But I *had* just seen a tiny man. Wearing a suit.

Maybe my suspicions that magic existed were true. Sometimes I daydreamed that if I just thought hard enough; just knew the right things to think or say, I could make something magical happen. Sometimes when I looked at the stars I felt they were looking back—that they were sentient. I was drawn to them like the sailors of old, and felt their pull as sure as gravity's.

But there was no way people evolved from animals other than apes. Hell, it was a miracle I believed in evolution at all. Since childhood it had been ingrained in me that evolution didn't exist. That 'Man has always walked Earth as we do now,' and 'God made Adam and Eve in his own likeness' was drilled into my head from the time I could talk. In high school my science teacher refused to teach us the subject of evolution. I'll never forget the day he said, "Class, the next chapter is on the theory of evolution. You can read it yourselves but I won't, as a Christian, teach it."

You bet I read that chapter. What's more, I became a science major.

I sat in stunned silence in the coffee shop; this time deep in thought. My erratic breathing had slowed, but my mind continued to race. The idea of Thayer and its people was completely enthralling. I had always been a little odd. I was the girl that drew unicorns on her notebook—the one who looked for rainbows and spun in circles on the playground. Normal girls dream of their wedding day, but not me. I always wondered who I would be, not whose bride. I never really fit in.

Not to mention my overwhelming fascination with the stars and astronomy. *Could some alternate universe have been calling to me?* I wondered. *Was there a whole other half of me that I had yet to discover?*

"So, you're saying my father..." I trailed off, not sure how to finish the thought.

"I have done some initial research into your background, Stella. I could find no connection between your mother, Elena, and Thayer. Stands to reason that your heritage is derived from your father, but I could find no record identifying him. I'd hoped you could help with that information."

"Well, that's going to be a problem. I never knew my father, and my mother refuses to speak of him."

The last time I asked about my father was for a genetics assignment in high school biology. Mom completely ignored my questions, ran to her bedroom swiping at her eyes, and stayed there until morning. The woman had always been prone to prayer, but I could hear her crying out for hours. The next morning she made breakfast as if nothing had happened. I let it go.

"Surely she would be more forthcoming if you asked her now," Gresham said. "You're twenty-two years old. An adult, though barely."

I snorted and shot him a 'barely this' look. I saw no reason for being condescending about my age again.

"I'll be twenty-three in August. And I'm telling you, she's kept this secret my entire life. I don't think she'll come around, but I'm willing to try, if for no other reason than to put all this nonsense to rest."

I looked out the window and noticed that Lizzie had pulled up outside the coffee shop. If I wanted to make my final, I had to hurry. We made plans to meet again that evening. I needed some time to soak all of this new information in. It wasn't every day a girl learned of an alternate utopia with dwarfs and magic.

It was even more infrequent that she learned she belonged in that world.

"Hi, Mom. Whatcha doin'?"

"Hi, babe. Well, the Church Beautiful committee meets today. We're planting azaleas in front of the Family Life Center. I was grabbin' my work gloves when I heard the phone. Everything okay?"

"Oh, fine, fine. Just talking to Lizzie about her mom and dad coming up for graduation. Made me think of my own father and what he's missing. You think he'd be interested to know I'm graduating college, Mom?"

I heard her grunt involuntarily, as if I'd punched her in the gut. She was silent for a long moment, but finally found her voice.

"I've got to go, darlin'," she began, but I cut her off.

"Mother! I'm a big girl. I can take it. There's no reason you can't tell me at least something about my father."

"I'm sorry. I can't be late for this meeting. I'll call you later."

"I don't care how bad it is, just tell me the truth." I yelled into the phone, taking my frustration out on the empty line long after she was gone.

A

The rest of the day turned out to be one of those that you look back on and wonder where the entire thing went. I daydreamed about the morning's revelation during every spare moment...and most moments I didn't have to spare.

Then I saw it happen before it happened. Most people I know have experienced deja vu, but it wasn't that. It played behind my eyes like an old-fashioned movie reel, flickering and shaky; the picture grainy and streaked. And then it happened.

One minute Dr. Charlton stood before the class, pointing at a Hertzsprung-Russell Diagram in preparation for the final, and the next he backhanded his chai all over the lecture hall desk and a disorderly stack of manila folders.

I risked a look at my classmates. Everyone was behaving normally. Looked like I was the only one who had watched the event play out twice. I wished I could say that was the first time, but it wasn't. Not even close.

I somehow got through my final, though I have no idea how well I did. I don't remember a single answer. I was preoccupied with thoughts of my father, the possibility of an ancient unknown world, of unexplainable premonitions, and about the impending meeting with Gresham, who had offered to pick me up since I was officially rideless.

I still had a lot of questions. I hadn't accepted the entirety of what he'd told me, but I was anxious to know more. Nothing wrong with gathering information in order to make an informed decision. Every time I blew off Gresham's revelation as the ravings of a madman I remembered the small suited man. No doubt that's why he brought him. Tricky, very tricky, this Gresham.

I used hot rollers so my thick red hair curled down my back. A little lipstick and mascara were all I ever wore for makeup, and I applied those before slipping into a billowy green top and a mustard skirt. I swiped Lizzie's peep-toe pumps and headed for the door. I expected Gresham at seven, and would really have preferred not to have him in the apartment again because, in hindsight, I was embarrassed about my vicious behavior. I was justified, to be sure, but still preferred not to relive the moment.

Gresham pulled into the apartment parking lot in a sleek gray European car and held the passenger door open for me after a quick hello. Once inside the car he glanced my way and put his hand on the gearshift. But then he looked at me again in that way—the predatory one from the day before that made me feel exposed.

I'm something of an odd genetic composition. While my moss green eyes are typical for a redhead, my skin isn't fair or freckled. It is olive, so it looks like an Italian was thrown in a blender with a Scotsman. He spent some time studying my face, and my eyes, especially, but it didn't escape my notice that he also lingered just a little too long on my shiny lips and barely-exposed knees. Men.

Some small part of me was glad that he was studying me with such fervor because it gave me a chance to rake him from head to toe unnoticed. He was wearing a suit and looked amazing. In college, in a college town, it was rare that I saw anyone in a suit. This was a real treat. When they fit right, like this one did, I think men look absolutely stunning in a suit. His was charcoal gray and very expensive. My guess was Italian. A crisp white shirt and small-patterned tie completed the ensemble that I was willing to bet was unmatched in town that night. His hair was different than when I first saw him. He'd arranged it so the black waves were more controlled, forced up and back. The result looked sophisticated, sexy. His eyes were even more striking than I recalled. The brilliant amber was unhindered by his muted suit and understated car. It was almost as if everything else was an elaborate setting for them.

I came back to the present, all too aware that my mouth had parted as I stared dreamily at him. I cleared my throat and looked away, but not fast enough to miss the amusement that flitted across his face.

He pulled out of the lot. Neither of us had said a thing since getting into the car. Was this sexual tension? I realized, horrified, that for me at least it was. I shook my head. He was too old and honestly too…something else I couldn't put my finger on. Dangerous? Predatory? Besides, he had made it very clear he thought I was much too young. Wait, why was I even having this internal debate? *Eyes on the prize, Stella, and he ain't it.* Information. That was the order of business for the night.

"What kind of food do you like?" I asked to get the conversation rolling. We hadn't discussed dinner, and I knew he was unfamiliar with the area.

"I made reservations at Luca. Do you know it?"

I did. Luca was an intimate, locally-owned Italian place with great atmosphere. It happened to be my favorite, though I rarely had an opportunity—well, the budget—to go.

After we were seated at a private table, the waiter took our drink order. Gresham ordered a bottle of French Blanc that was way out of my league. If I ever splurged at all I went for the $8 glass instead of the $6.50. I hadn't had anything of that caliber and I told him so.

"Life's too short for cheap wine and expensive women, I always say," Gresham smiled.

His joke lightened the mood a bit, and we fell into easy conversation about the town and about food. I ordered the seafood risotto and Gresham asked for the same.

"Can I do anything else for you, sir?" the waiter asked. There had been a definite emphasis on 'else.' I glanced up at him just in time to see his attempt at smoldering, but the look wasn't meant for me. I cleared my throat, but the waiter spared me no attention.

"Henri," with a thicker Southern drawl than mine, was paying far too much attention to Mr. Gresham. Each time he offered to serve Gresham in some way, the waiter looked at the floor and bit his lip.

"I think you have an admirer," I said grinning from ear to ear.

"Who? Henri?" Gresham pronounced it 'ahn REE' as opposed to the 'HEN ree' that I suspected he was given at birth. "Oh, he's cute, but not my type."

A record scratched in my brain. Was Gresham gay? Maybe he was. The suit, the hair, the shoes, the emphatic insistence I was in no danger from his advances… Highly possible when I looked at it from that angle. Dayum, what a shame. He would make such beautiful little black-haired baby Greshams. But then how could his reaction to me in my apartment be explained? This topic definitely required further investigation.

"I realize you probably have a lot of questions, Stella, and I'm happy to answer as many as I can. Did you get any information from your mother?"

"Ah, no. I asked her on the phone but, as expected, she changed the subject and hung up. I'll ask her again this Saturday when she's in town for my graduation."

"Graduation. Right. From the university," he said, suddenly preoccupied. "That does present a problem. I had hoped to take you to Thayer this weekend. I'd planned to leave first thing Saturday morning."

My brain short-circuited in shock, and my stomach threatened to return the expensive wine. It was one thing to discuss an alternate realm and wax poetic about its throwback lifestyle. It was quite another to accept that it actually existed. And then to entertain the thought of physically entering said realm…well, that was just insane.

My mind vomited questions. Was he for real? Was I actually buying into this whole thing? If so, was I really considering going? Could I come back? Was it dangerous? How would I get there? What would I pack? All of these questions flew through my mind as I absorbed what Gresham had proposed.

The one I asked was, "What's the rush?"

He smiled. "As I told you before, being part-Thayerian has likely resulted in your possessing talents—of a supernatural nature. You've possessed them your entire life, but for safety reasons they've been concealed from your knowledge. Their use has been restricted until you're old enough to control them. They're yours by birthright, but you must be mature enough to use discretion and good judgment."

That little tidbit blew my mind. I had a magical talent? What was it? I took a sip of my water and didn't know if the slickness on the glass was condensation, or the result of my nerves.

"What about children born in Thayer? Both....two-dimensional...and full-blooded Thayerian? Are their abilities suspended until they reach maturity, too? What exactly is the age of maturity? Is it standard and arbitrary like voting or drinking?"

"Though there aren't many, we prefer to call people like you bi-dimensional. Two-dimensional implies a lack of depth." He smirked.

I twisted my lips, nonplussed. He cleared his throat and continued, "The answer to your question is yes. The use of supernatural abilities is restricted until age twenty-one. But the age is not exactly arbitrary; it's believed by scientists, both in your world and mine, that the brain doesn't fully mature until the mid-twenties. This of course varies from species to species in my world, but our governing bodies came to a consensus at twenty-one. Just imagine a gang of preteens with superpowers. They wouldn't survive into adulthood. Many didn't, which is the reason for such restrictions."

"Sure, that makes sense, I guess," I said, though it did *not* make sense. "But what now? How will I even know what my powers are? Can I just start practicing in the bathroom or what? Maybe I don't even have any."

"No," he laughed. "While you may have already felt some changes or experienced unexplainable urges, your full abilities will only manifest in Thayer. And even then only with guidance and lots of practice."

My sudden recollection of the previous day's premonitory weirdness must have shown on my face because Gresham leaned in, an excited gleam in his eyes.

"You've already felt something, haven't you?"

I gave a noncommittal 'mmm' and looked away.

"I knew it," he said, pleasure adding color across his sharp cheekbones. "I want to leave Saturday because a primos class starts Monday at Radix, Thayer's Citadel for Supernatural Learning."

I quirked a brow at the name.

"It's a beautiful campus built centuries ago," he said. "And an unparalleled educational experience."

"What does 'primos' mean?" I asked.

"It's our term for entering students. Instead of freshman, in Thayer they're called primos—primos, sophos, tertios, quartos. Radix is a less American university-type atmosphere than you're accustomed to here…more of a magical training ground for adult students."

"I see the appeal, Mr. Gresham. I really do. But, why me? And how did you find me?"

"I've been trying to find you for some time, but it's been difficult. I suspected that you were out there somewhere, but only recently discovered where. That's why I was so thrilled to hear you say your name, despite the circumstances. My long search was over."

"Huh," I said, still thoroughly creeped out that he'd known to look for me. I had a bad feeling about the whole thing. "Sorry," I said, declining his invitation to leave my comfy world. "My graduation ceremony doesn't mean a lot to me, to be honest, but it does to my mother. I should cross the stage with my class."

"That's all right," he said, undeterred. "Are you free tomorrow?"

I must have been out of my mind. I was leaving the only world I had ever known for another filled with magic and mystical species. I'd had to lie to my roommate and say that I was going out of town for a job interview. I hated lying, but how could I reveal something as outlandish as what I was attempting to do? She would never believe me even if I did tell her, and according to Gresham, the fewer people outside of Thayer that knew of its existence the better. I would be back in town in time for graduation, and none would be the wiser.

I lay awake the night before entertaining the idea that Thayer existed. I weighed pros and cons; tried to make an informed decision. On the one hand, I had proof mystical beings did exist in the form of a dapper little bearded man. Also, and this was a stretch, but perhaps my precognitive experiences that had been growing more frequent of late might be the suppressed abilities to which Gresham referred. Finally, I really wanted everything Gresham had told me to be true. It would explain my lifelong tendency toward the weird. It could explain the useless scratchy visions. And I could finally get some information about my father.

Cons? The whole thing could be a construct of a handsome stranger's demented mind…although, that wouldn't explain the gnome. Thayer could actually exist, but wasn't safe, and I would be in danger the moment I set foot there. Gresham could have an ulterior motive in taking me to this new world. Hell, his primary motive wasn't real clear. He could be the one I should fear. But if he meant me harm, he could easily have taken me somewhere by force that day in my apartment. No, he wanted me to go to Thayer willingly, and he wanted me to like it.

It might be dangerous, but I was willing to risk it. The potential pros far outweighed the cons, and I was excited to see Thayer.

A

"Good morning," said a clean-shaved Gresham. "I hope you slept well, despite the anticipation of what awaits you today."

Gresham was waiting outside my apartment door sporting a grin as I grabbed my sweater and a small suitcase. He was super chipper, which I found...odd. His morning glow was quite a change from the subdued Mr. Rigid I'd encountered before. Maybe he was excited to be going home. He looked fantastic and completely put together in low-slung flat-front black pants and a lightweight charcoal sweater. My eyes snagged briefly on the way his hipbones protruded above the band of his pants. Wide shoulders paired with that narrow waistline made me wonder what he looked like without a shirt.

I was staring. Again. I snapped to attention, raising eyelids that had drooped as my imagination got busy. I shook myself and noticed with confusion that Gresham's gaze was still on my lips.

I cleared my throat and answered the man's question because at that moment it was all I could think to do.

"Actually, I lay awake for hours imagining what Thayer looks like, what the people look like, and hell, what they will think of me. After that I tossed and turned wondering who my father is and if I'll ever meet him. Then just before dawn I dozed off only to wake grabbing the sheets and gasping for breath after a horrifying dream that I'd been defragmented like an old computer while attempting to cross realms."

I fidgeted with the strap of my bag. I was practically bouncing with nervous energy. "I'm babbling. Sorry. How do we do this? Is there a top-secret teleporter? Some hidden ley line? Oh. I know—an ancient dolmen marked by megaliths. Or is there some heightened state of awareness that we need to achieve first? Don't worry; I have read the books and seen the movies. I am well educated in all sorts of inter-dimensional transportation methods."

Gresham's mindset appeared to have gone from cheerful to leashed tolerance. Must not be a fan of the fantasy genre.

He took a deep breath and shook his head. "No, no, none of that. It's much simpler, actually. Just think of where you want to go, take a step in that direction, and you'll arrive at your intended destination."

My incomprehension must have been evident because he added, "There are limitations, of course. Travel by intention is limited to a desired physical location, rather than specific person. You cannot just think 'I want Matilder' and appear on the sofa beside her. Most Thayerians create barriers, or wards, around their property so that guests aren't just popping into their bedroom any time they please."

I glazed over at some point. This was all so…so unlikely.

"Since you haven't been to Thayer and can't imagine a specific physical location, I'll lead us both. Give me your hand."

I looked to his outstretched hand. My mind was stuck on 'take a step in that direction.' I tried to speak, but only soft grunts escaped. I was suddenly dizzy, and I widened my stance so that I didn't topple over. Hot May air ran over the back of my tongue as I closed my eyes and breathed deeply, willing myself calm and open-minded.

"You can do this, Stella," he said with authority.

I swallowed past the lump in my throat. "I can do this. I can do this. I can do this," I whispered. I placed my free hand in his warm—no, just plain hot—hand, and held onto my luggage with the other. He gave a slight, reassuring squeeze and nodded once at me.

Ready or not…

My eyes, which had been squinted shut, flew open at the sensations that permeated my entire being. My body was moving much too fast for my mind to comprehend. Unable to see or do anything else, I leaned into Gresham and grabbed his forearm with my free hand. I squinted my eyes again and lay my forehead on his shoulder, gritting my teeth in disabling fear and wishing desperately for the moment that the whole thing was over. There was a brief severe cold, like a container of dry ice had been opened. No rushing wind or intricate light tubes. One moment I was outside my apartment and the next I was…somewhere else.

Before me stood a colossal stone gateway that opened onto a campus straight out of a pictorial guide to Gothic architecture.

I had just traveled by intention

I stood sucking breath after breath, making an effort—
and failing—to regain my composure. My wobbly legs
melted completely when I pried my fingers from my escort's
arm, so I bent and braced my hands on my knees until the
moment passed. Gresham, though, looked as if we'd just
stepped through any other doorway. Traveling to another
world using only the power of thought? No big.

"Aha," he said and threw his arms open wide. "Here we
are. Welcome to Radix, Citadel for Supernatural Learning. Or,
as the students more commonly refer to it, 'The Root.' "

I dropped my bag and craned my head to take in the sights
before me. The grounds were lush and pristine with vibrant
green grass forming cushy mounds between flowerbeds
overflowing with blooms. Bountiful vines of ivy grew up
massive stone structures and billowed over arching entryways.
The muted natural stone buildings and slate roofs contrasted
beautifully with the lush, vivid gardens and the brilliant blue
sky.

When we left my apartment building it was a temperate
Southern May morning. It seemed to be about the same in
Thayer. I made a mental note to ask Gresham if the

temperatures here varied with geography, as they did in my world.

"Shall we?" Gresham extended his elbow, like I was Scarlett to his Rhett and should curtsy and take his arm.

"Did we go back in time, too, or just a parallel universe?"

I regretted the comment as soon as it left my mouth. It sounded way snarkier coming out than it did in my head, and Gresham's disappointed expression left me feeling like a real asshole.

"I think you'll find many things different in Thayer," he said. "The employment of simple graciousness and self-censorship are among the first two I hope you'll absorb."

His fatherly tone stung worse because he was right. I resolved not to be such a shit, but admitted it was going to be a tough row to hoe.

"I'm sorry. I'm nervous. Where to now?"

Gresham scowled, dubious that my regret was sincere.

"Oh, please?" I pleaded. "I really am sorry." I put the full force of my apology in my eyes and he nodded before moving on smoothly…graciously.

"I thought we'd tour the grounds first. Then perhaps you could meet a few students you'll be joining…er, the class that begins Monday."

Gresham's slip opened doors better left closed. Sure, I was anxious to see this new magical world, but the thought of leaving my home for this one, at least temporarily, was altogether different. What about my mother? My friends? My life? I couldn't just pick up and leave everything behind. I didn't know a soul in Thayer. I didn't know the culture. Hell, I didn't know if it was safe. I had no idea what the school would be like, or who I really was—that much was clear.

Having just finished college, I had no desire to cram for tests again. And the place looked like it cost a fortune. I could never pay for something like that. These thoughts raced through my head, but my body had gone stiff as death. Gresham sensed my panic and cursed himself beneath his breath.

"I'm sorry. I've put the cart before the horse. There's no pressure to attend Radix. Today is just an introduction into a world that may be yours. Let's tour the campus and have some lunch."

Baby steps. Immediate planning only. I knew what he was doing. But it worked and I nodded, put my brave face on, and stepped through the gate separating Radix from the rest of Thayer.

A

After a tour of the administration building I learned that Radix was much more than a school for people like me who were learning to develop their inherent abilities. The system was made up of smaller colleges of study, a research and development wing, and a combat school, though it was unclear to me whether magical or hand-to-hand type warfare was taught. There was even a career development institute, and a brig. It was for magical bad boys, I supposed. The property was large enough to accommodate the many buildings, but I never would've known by the feel of the homey campus.

Gresham led me toward a building that I had admired earlier. The mammoth yellow-gray stone structure was 'L'-shaped, and its large central entrance featured a real-life castle turret. Radix seemed to be built with defensive precautions in mind. The thick stone walls surrounding the campus and the turrets suggested as much.

"This building is just stunning," I said, bouncing from foot to foot. "What is it?"

I'd been drawn to the building from the moment I saw it. I was dying to go inside, to climb ancient stone stairs, and to view the campus from the medieval perch.

Gresham appeared pleased with my enthusiasm and shot me a mischievous look. He bit down on his lip and raised eyebrows at me in silent dare.

"This formidable structure is one many a Radix Alumnus has called home. Sabre Hall is the residential facility for most students. Would you like to go inside?"

Gresham was so strikingly handsome and I was so giddy with excitement that I very nearly grabbed him by the back of the head and pulled him close enough to bite that lip myself.

Wait, what?

I took a deep breath. Concentrated on calming down. My senses had obviously been overcome with the revelation of a new world, of this spectacular institution, of a new perspective. The excitement of it all had gotten to me. I had to keep a level head about me so I could make an informed, rational decision.

Oh, to hell with it.

I giggled and nearly ran toward the turreted entrance, noticing for the first time the heavenly scent of honeysuckle-type vine draped over the wide wooden doors.

As I tried to swing the heavy door inward, I met complete resistance. I looked for a door pull instead, but found none. With hands on my hips I stepped back and shook my head, puzzled at just how I was supposed to enter Sabre Hall.

I heard Gresham give a little chuckle and swung around to see what was so funny.

"Allow me." He rested his hand on the dark-colored wood and it silently drifted open.

"It's bespelled," he said. "Only Sabre Hall residents can enter, though as your...advisor of sorts, I have access."

Stepping across the threshold into Sabre Hall was like stepping into another time. My eyes were immediately drawn to the vertical expanse of the grand hall. It was at least four stories high and ovular in shape. Each floor had a gleaming oak balustrade that provided a connection to the grand hall. The feel was inclusive, open.

Centuries-old oil portraits lined the walls, as did brilliant landscapes and even some mythical-looking creatures, beautiful in their fearsomeness.

As I silently walked the perimeter of the room, absorbing the old world ambiance and falling in love with the architecture, the art, and even the oriental rugs, I stopped at one cracked and weathered painting. Something about the creature depicted mesmerized me. It was in mid-chase, its powerful front legs digging into the ground for traction as its back legs extended behind as if preparing to push into another potent stride. Though it was running across the canvas, its head was turned so that the full weight of its menacing gaze jumped off of the painting. I stepped back and lay a hand across my chest. Those eyes. So fearsome, so violent, so intelligent. A wolf. A massive, beautiful black wolf that must have existed lifetimes ago, as evidenced by the antique frame and cracked paint.

"These paintings…this place is magical. I'm afraid I got lost in the moment." I struggled to peel my gaze from the painting, and turned to Gresham, who still stood behind me.

"I'm glad you like it here. It suits you, I think. Would you like to…"

Whatever he said I didn't hear because behind him, where no one had been before, the Sabre Grand Hall had begun to bustle with life.

At first I noticed people who looked like me. They hauled luggage, boxes, tiny refrigerators. Others talked and laughed. The harder I looked, though, the more my brain processed what I was seeing.

The people looked like me, but not like me. A girl closest to me gave a whole new meaning to 'doe eyed.' She really, truly, had eyes like a deer. Large and black, they were framed by long, straight lashes, and she blinked in excess. The most stunning thing about her, though, was her ears. The velvety pointed things protruded from her head maybe four inches. Cute little tiny ears the same color as her dark honey hair twitched as though she were picking up and assessing every sound in the hall. And maybe she was. She caught me staring and I tried quickly, though I suspected unconvincingly, to smile and appear polite. She smiled back, gave me a quick blink and nodded her head in hello.

My gaze snagged on a guy sitting in a dark brown leather club chair moving his fingers over a miniature computer tablet. It was not his ears that caused me to stare, but his feet. Bare, they were long and a brownish green that was unmistakably....amphibian. Spotted and jointed, they made me think "salamander."

Everywhere I turned, there were both people who I could have passed on the sidewalk back home, and those with foreign body compositions. I felt weak-kneed and needed to sit down. This was obviously what Gresham meant when he said in Thayer people evolved from many origins, not just primates.

Oddly enough, I wasn't afraid of anyone bustling about the hall, and some were quite scary looking. Rather, I was in awe of the wondrous place and its people. The building was teeming with life. The excitement and the anticipation were almost palpable. It was infectious, and I had a pang of jealousy that the adventure wasn't mine.

"What are the dorm rooms like?" I asked Gresham, still gawking but trying not to get caught.

"They're small but comfortable, if memory serves. Single-occupancy. Shared bathrooms. Adequate, I suppose."

"Hmmm. So I'd have a suite mate. You think she'd be human-looking like me, or someone whose ancestors swam the seas?"

"I have no idea, Stella, but I like hearing you talk like this." His smile was as wolf-like as the painting I'd admired.

"Oh, I'm just dreaming, Gresham, don't look so pleased with yourself. One thing I've been wondering, though. Do all these people get along, or does...not racism...specie-ism exist here? Is that a word?"

He started to answer, but I cut him off. "My god, this place is fascinating. Let's see the rest of it." Feeling more and more at ease, I took the lead, heading in the direction that people seemed to be coming and going.

"Do you like espresso? That's where you are headed. There's a bar through those doors. Coffee during the day and a full bar at night."

"Are you freaking kidding me? A dorm with a bar? Pinch me now."

"It isn't a dorm. It's a residence hall for adult students. We're all adults here."

"What do you mean? What's the difference?"

"Well, no one cares whether or not you sneak boys into your room for one thing. For another, no one is monitoring your alcohol consumption. Forgive me for being indelicate, but you can close the place down and take home the bartender, and no one will care."

It was definitely my kind of place. How great to have some beers with your friends and stumble upstairs? Then back down for your morning caffeine needs.

"Forgive me for being indelicate…'" I mimicked playfully. "Lighten up, Gresham. You're not going to scandalize me, I assure you."

"If you knew me better, you wouldn't make such foolish declarations. I could scandalize you with one smack of your pink ass."

My lips parted with shock and I stared numbly before muttering, "Touché, Gresham…touché."

We pushed through a pair of ancient oak doors and stepped into an old-fashioned gentlemen's club. The room's comfortable warmth permeated my senses at once. Lit only by sparse sconces and art lights to display more paintings, the room's feature was a crackling fireplace big enough to walk through. Supple leather chairs and booths were spaced around the fireplace, as were over-sized ottomans better suited as seats than for feet. Dark wood wainscoting met sophisticated gray paint. I followed the walls up, and saw crown molding with detail beyond any I'd seen in my provincial upbringing. The whole place screamed privilege and class and I should have felt out of my element. But I didn't. Surrounded by the fire's warmth and the faint aromas of smoke and hops I felt at home.

Opposite the fireplace was a stunning carved-wood bar. The panels, the columns, the top were all sculpted into an enormous dragon inlaid with precious stones. Intelligent emerald eyes loomed beneath the dragon's heavy brow. A fierce scaly tail ornate with rubies seemed to whip from pillars at the bar's flanks.

In addition to the dragon, gnomes and demure-looking fairies were carved in the panels. The creatures' faces were so life-like that I reached out to touch them. I lay fingers on the cheek of a particularly desolate-looking fairy and ran the pad of my thumb across the line of her brow. Her eyes were too large for her face to be a human. She looked childlike, but those eyes were the mature, knowing eyes of a woman. Not just a woman; a woman who had known pain. There was a hopelessness to her that made my heart ache. It was a remarkable rendering and I had never seen such poignant artistry. I felt raw, emotional. I wanted a glass of wine, not coffee.

"S'more than woodwork, Jeenjah, it tells a story, ken?"

"Wha?" I looked around for the speaker.

"This bar gives a face to history, though a pretty history tis'nt."

I looked up, blinking, to see who owned that voice, and realized with a jerk that he had been so bold as to call me "Ginger," a moniker I wasn't especially fond of.

The bartender lifted a horizontally-latched portion of the bar up and made his way inside. He was taller than me, but not by much. His fine, sandy blond hair tossed about his head with a carelessness also found in his dress. His linen shirt was untucked and fell over khaki shorts. I couldn't see his feet, but my guess was worn boat shoes with no laces.

"Welcome. Folks call me Knox. I run this place. Can I get ya somethin'?" His voice held something like a Scottish burr— ken I git yeh soompthin.

"Stella. I'm Stella. What story do the carvings tell?"

"A sad story. And a true one. A long time ago, a ruthless sorcerer desired more power, more land…he wanted to rule Thayer and to harness the power of its people. 'Twas widely known then, as it is now, that the gnomes and fairies hold the keys to nature, to crops and harvests, and even to the seasons. The sorcerer believed if he controlled Thayer's flora and climate he could starve out our people, our rulers, and overtake our lands. He viciously attacked the gnomes and fairies. He ferreted out all he could find using dragons to set fire to the forests and fields they called home. He killed so many...so many."

Knox paused as if it was a struggle to continue the story. He still looked in my direction, but he no longer saw me. His eyes had become shiny, distant. I began to fidget, and nervously cleared my throat. He blinked, looked at me as if he'd forgotten I was there, and smiled once more. The sad little moment was over.

"The sorcerer's plan failed in the end," he went on, "despite slaughtering the majority of the Gnome and Fae people, he never obtained the power to influence nature."

"No?" I asked dreamily.

I was engrossed in his story. He had a particularly brilliant ability to make a connection, one I felt keenly. He was probably a very popular bartender.

"No," he said. "You see, in his arrogance, what the wizard didn't understand is that the wee people never controlled the seasons or our plant life. They're merely stewards. They possessed the magic to tend the lands, and were honored to do so. But when their numbers fell so tragically the magic fell to Thayer itself, whose citizens took up the task."

As he told the story, he'd made his way to stand across the bar from me, and leaned across the wood to rub his thumb up and down my arm. He circled the underside of my wrist with each down stroke light as a feather. I'd become so absorbed in the story and was so intently studying the etchings in the wood that I hadn't even realized he was doing it. I pulled my hand away, scowling, not sure if I was upset at myself for becoming so easily bespelled or at him for touching me so intimately when we were so *not* intimate.

My rebuff didn't seem to faze him, because he only backed away and picked up a dishtowel to dry a pint glass, continuing his story without a hitch.

"Over time, the Gnome and Fae who survived repopulated and eventually the magic of harvest, and of nature itself, returned to its rightful stewards."

"What a tragic story," I breathed. "But such a beautiful ending."

I thought of the small man Gresham had brought to the coffee shop as proof of Thayer's existence and supernatural nature. I wanted to know the gnome better. And I wanted to meet a fairy. I had so much to learn.

"I'm sorry," I said as an afterthought. "What's a Fae?"

He looked at me as if I'd sprouted ears of my own and turned his head from side to side as he tried to figure me out.

"You are new here, aren'tcha Ginger?"

"Ha. Yes, quite," I evaded. "Tell me, what happened to the dragons?"

"All gone. The people of Thayer went to war in retribution for the stewards' massacre. Not a dragon's been seen since then. We got them all."

"And the sorcerer?"

"He lives. None know where. Many suspect he waits in hiding, in anticipation of the day he once again tries to overtake Thayer. But dinna fash, Ginger, we'll be ready for him this time. And he's got no dragons."

"My name is Stella," I said with force. "And you can't tell me that a sorcerer who lived centuries ago is still alive somewhere. People don't live that long."

"Aye, they do. Just ask your bodyguard here. Why, he's been a—"

"Thank you, Knox, for that fascinating account of our tragic history," growled Gresham, who until then had been markedly absent from our conversation. I hadn't noticed his absence, but at that point he crossed the room to me.

"I'm sure your efforts were really paying off, right up to the point you insulted her. You're slipping. Better work on your delivery."

Gresham grabbed me by the elbow and urged me out of the bar area.

"We're leaving."

Knox's eyes held mischief and he gave a sly grin.

"Goodbye, Stella. If you manage to shake this old boring one, you know where to find me."

After nodding his head toward Gresham so that there was no question who he found so boring, Knox winked at me. The face that first held that mischievous grin then took on a more determined look. I got the feeling that there was a back-story between him and Gresham.

Gresham overly-forcefully deposited me through the double doors, and I swung around to face him.

"What crawled up your ass and died?" I demanded.

He just looked at me, blank-faced, and blinked. Then blinked again.

It's just an idiom. Oh, never mind. Good god, Gresham, do you even have a sense of humor?"

Mr. Tall, Dark and Menacing puffed up. "Oh!" he said, affronted. "I have a sense of humor... And I am a lot of fun, I'll have you know."

That, I seriously doubted. He had the whole sexy and mysterious thing going for him, but I couldn't see him cracking jokes, much less throwing back cold ones with the guys or hitting the dance floor.

"What was that all about with you and Knox, anyway? That was a seriously bad vibe."

"I have known Knox Mahon for a very long time. He considers himself the ultimate ladies' man. I place a high value on honor, and I...I find he has none."

"Yeah, I get that. But why would his predilections have such a violent effect on you? What did he do that was so dishonorable?"

That was a question he did not want to address, because he gritted his teeth, the flexing of his jaw muscles a visible indicator of his irritation. "I have some business to attend across campus," he said. "I thought you might like to get to know a few students. Do you mind if I leave you in the common room, the Grand Hall, for a while?"

Though his moods were giving me whiplash, I didn't object. In fact, I looked forward to exploring on my own.

A

I found my way to the upper levels of the building...castle...whatever, and aimlessly wandered the halls. This was so like college, but so *un*like college. It was almost as if graduate students had taken over a dorm—less evidence of binge drinking and more evidence of study, more meaningful conversation.

The people seemed to have it together better than I did. I was gonna have to step up my game if I wanted to fit in.

I realized with a start that some part of me did want to fit in at Radix. I'd always been an outsider, a wandering mess in search of a home, but learning of Thayer, of Radix, and of the possibility I belonged here made me want something more than I had in a very long time. Maybe ever.

I wanted to belong at Radix because I suspected I already did. The moment I stepped foot inside the ancient gates of Radix an invisible rope wound around my heart and pulled me toward it. With each bit of information about the school, each glimpse into its history, each encounter with a student the rope drew me closer and closer to becoming a student at The Root. To becoming a Thayerian citizen. My heart fluttered nervously at the life-altering realization. But no panic attack approached.

I wasn't sure I could leave my mother. What would I tell her? And, committing to more school when I hadn't yet graduated didn't hold great appeal,but the mere thought of being a student at Radix was intoxicating. The day before I'd had no idea what to do with my life. Today, enrolling at Radix seemed the most natural decision in the world.

I stumbled upon an open common area with over-sized leather loungers and a kitchenette. Doe Eyes' willowy legs were curled beneath her in a chair as she read a fashion magazine. She was wearing a long, loose beige sweater, stretchy brown leggings, and tall buckskin boots. She made lovely look effortless. I hated her immediately.

"Hi, I'm Stella," I said as I approached her and gave a little wave. "This is my first time here."

"Timbra Redfern," she said and stood to her full height, which was at least five foot nine. She had an easy smile, but only made brief eye contact as she crossed her arms, tucking her hands between biceps and body. She hunched forward a bit, too. Her shyness surprised me. I hated her a little less.

"So, you're the one everyone is talking about," she said, still smiling.

"Talking? About me? Who knows I'm here?" The revelation I was the topic of conversation gave me a jolt of panic. I'd never wanted to be the center of attention. In fact, I had always done my best to stay on the outskirts of it.

"Oh. Just everyone," she said. "Trust me, the moment you stepped foot on campus, speculation began. I heard that even a couple of bets were placed on the spot. Odds are you won't last a week. No one can remember the last time a bi-dimensional came through. Ours is a big world, but it's still small town."

Perfect. Probably before I had even decided to stay myself, half the campus was betting against me. But, god knew, as the only little girl in my tiny school whose daddy was unaccounted for, I had plenty of experience as the subject of gossip. I had also always been one to rise to a challenge.

"Well, I'm afraid even a week is too long for their bets. There's no way I can afford this place, even if I wanted to stay. I took out loans for what scholarships didn't cover of undergrad back home."

"Afford?" Timbra squinted at me. "Tuition and board at Radix…even a monthly stipend are all covered by Thayer. We're considered investments as citizens, as future guardians. If you're lucky enough to be accepted, Stella, you don't have to pay anything."

"Oh," was all I could manage.

I considered what life in a college town had to offer me, and couldn't come up with anything that drew my interest. I thought about moving back into my mother's house. She would be happy if I lived at home for the rest of my life—just as long as I accompanied her to church every time two or more were gathered. Good lord, the thought of that. I could see our future together just like two Edies from Gray Gardens, one just as batshit crazy as the other, bickering all day about patè and cats.

I had always suspected there was something else out there for me, some greater purpose, and I knew in my bones that Radix and Thayer were it. I might as well dig my heels in and plant some roots. With this hearty dose of resolve warming me from the inside, I knew forward was the only way to go.

"I enjoyed meeting you, Timbra," I said. Then the words were out of my mouth before I could scoop them back in. "I need to find Admissions. Classes start Monday and I haven't even bought books."

Big brown eyes held a knowing twinkle. "Ha. I knew I liked you. Tell them you want the fourth floor. We can be neighbors."

*A*dmissions turned out to be not much different than in any other institute of higher learning. A drag-ass woman in her fifties somehow found the energy to help me register for classes and find a room. She left me with no doubt as to my ineptitude and inexperience in the world as a whole. *Worlds, plural,* I thought belatedly. I didn't know if I would ever get used to that. Despite the registrar I left the building with a positive outlook on the days ahead.

It was well past lunchtime and I was famished. After tossing the sophisticated PDA awarded to me upon registration into my bag, I found a campus map and Café Row.

Quite unlike any campus I'd been on, there was no stark cafeteria or food court. Instead, and much to my pleasure, a line of quaint bistros lined the elevated bank of a river that formed the back of Radix campus. A pizzeria, a sandwich shop, and others had placed bistro tables beneath brightly covered umbrellas. The view of the river was breathtaking and peaceful as I approached a counter to order a wood-fired margherita pizza and a glass of cabernet.

"I'll charge this to your account, Ms…"

"Stonewall. Stella."

"Ms. Stonewall. Nice to meet you. I'm Nick." Nick's worn, white apron sported yellow stains along the circumference of his portly belly—an obvious catch-all for his daily pizza making. He had kind eyes, a bulbous nose, and an easy smile. And he made a damn fine pizza.

I sat in contented silence for several minutes enjoying my simple meal and the borderline-naughty midday glass of wine. I was at peace with my decision to stay. It was right. Predestined even, and I laughed at the thought that not two days before I had no idea what I was going to do with my life.

It was at this moment, as I sat alone with a goofy grin on my face, that Rowan Gresham appeared across the table from me.

"Isn't it amazing the effect on one's perspective that can be made by a glass of wine and a moment's peace?" he asked.

I rather thought it was amazing the effect a glass of wine and a grumpy old dude could have on my libido, but no way was I telling him that.

Instead, I confidently slid a copper-colored folder emblazoned with the gleaming gold Radix logo across the bistro table.

He glanced at it, threw open the folder. "You did it," he breathed.

I couldn't be sure, but I thought that the look that passed over his features was a mixture of astonished pleasure and satisfaction. Then I realized it was pride. He was proud of me. My heart fluttered a little at the thought of pleasing him, but mostly I was pleased with myself for taking all of this new information in stride and moving forward.

My PDA buzzed and a studious-looking female avatar peered up at me from the screen.

A sultry female voice intoned, "Stella, the New Semester Mixer begins in two hours in Sabre Hall's ballroom."

The avatar was modeled after me.

"Er, thank you?" I wasn't sure if she could hear me, but thanked her just in case—I didn't want to hurt her feelings. Dang Southern genteel compulsions...

"It is my pleasure," she replied.

"It can hear me, then?" I turned to Gresham, who was interrupted before he could comment.

"It is sitting right here, and can hear you. You may call me Pia. I am a personal interactive assistant, and am assigned to you for the remainder of your time here at Radix. I control your schedule, can help with your orientation, and am a means of communication with your teachers and peers. I will also assist with, store, and submit any necessary coursework."

"Ah, all right," I said and shrugged before turning to Gresham, "You going to this thing? This mixer?"

"Not really my scene. I have a conflict anyway. But you should go. Meet some of your classmates."

"I think I will," I said, and my smile matched Gresham's.

"Congratulations, and welcome to The Root." He shocked me by running his arm behind my shoulders for a perfectly appropriate hug. Despite its propriety, the forced proximity to his big body was so new, so very warm that the blush on my cheeks was from more than the wine.

A

"Well, okay, Pia," I said after a moment. I don't suppose you know my room assignment at Sabre Hall? I have a party to get ready for."

I rolled my eyes in sarcasm and waved goodbye to Gresham, secretly delighting in my new toy.

"Of course I do. You will reside in Room 412. The mixer dress is smart casual."

"You're way cooler than Siri, Pia."

"I'm funnier, too."

"Oh yeah," I asked her. "Know any jokes?"

She replied, deadpan, "Three iPhones walk into a bar..."

A

One quick turn of a key gained entrance to my new home. I was delighted to find it came with worn but comfortable antique furnishings. A full-sized turned wood bed was covered with a quilt that had been washed so many times it fell limply into every crevice of the worn mattress. A simple table was an instant catchall for Pia and my badge.

The room smelled old, but in a homey way—of oiled wood and fresh linen, of worn leather and just a hint of lemon cleaning solution. A large dresser and an adequate closet—is any closet ever really big enough?—would provide space for my things, and I found a small buffet held exactly two wine glasses and two sets of dinnerware.

I lay my overnight bag at the foot of a leather chair upon an ancient but radiant wool rug. The dyed crimsons, ochres, and indigoes were still vibrant despite centuries of wear and tear. It was soft but firm beneath my toes, and I closed my eyes and lay my head back against the chair, stretching my neck and melting into my new home.

"Damn. Damn, damn, damn." This string of curses and muffled clanging alerted me to the existence of another door on the left side of the room. I opened it slowly, and discovered a visibly frustrated Timbra Redfern.

"Oh, it *is* you," she said. "I was trying to make some room in this bathroom cabinet. My room is just through there." She pointed to a door on the opposite side of the room.

We stood in a Jack and Jill-style bathroom with doors to our bedrooms at either end. While it was small, it had been recently updated, and had a double vanity and the clean lines of contemporary design. The chrome fixtures were muted and tasteful, but another wool rug provided a shock of color and comfort.

"What was all the "damning" about?" I asked Timbra, who had continued to make space within the cabinet for my things.

"Oh," she said, and looked up, embarrassed. "I'm all knees and elbows, you know, and can hardly turn around in here without breaking something."

This mental picture was too much, considering she was so...so...deer-like, and I could just picture a real deer in our bathroom slipping around on hooves, all knees and elbows like Bambi wearing stilettos on ice. I giggled, and when she ran an elbow into the door it erupted into a full-blown belly laugh, at which point she got over being affronted and simply joined in.

And there in our shared bathroom, with the audible sigh that accompanies the end of all belly laughs, we became friends.

Timbra helped me dress for the mixer, having a firm grasp of what the term "smart casual" represented. Between the few things I had packed and her particular talent with hair, makeup, and accessories, I almost approached presentable. In stretchy black jeans, a thinly striped top, black heels and gold jewelry, I felt pretty good about my first foray into Radix society.

This self-confidence lasted until Timbra met me in the hall. She was one of those people who always looked thin and perfectly put together. Being her friend was going to be tough.

*T*he two of us entered an already-populous ballroom, and while the looker beside me deserved all the attention, I knew all eyes were on me. Chill bumps skittered up my spine before my lungs seized. I stood unmoving, not breathing as paranoia fought with embarrassment.

Timbra nudged me and cleared her throat. When I still didn't move, she patted me on the shoulder and whispered, "You got this."

I inhaled deeply and fought to overcome my fright. I took another breath, then another, and eased back into my senses. Once the initial shock of being the center of attention, the new girl in a new world, wore off I resolved not to make it easier for anyone to reject me. I stood up a little straighter and headed for the bar with a confidence that was purely superficial. I ordered a glass of liquid courage in the form of a margarita, and Timbra had an Old Fashioned. Of course she did. Even her drink was a sophisticated throwback.

A DJ in the corner spun upbeat dance music, and after the initial collective gawk at the new girl, the crowd's conversations started back up. I had just begun to relax a little when a group of four approached us.

"Who's the new girl, Redfern?" an imposing man asked. He had to be at least six-five and I could tell by the rounded slope of his shoulders and the girth of his thighs that underneath a vintage concert T-shirt and jeans was a hulking mass of muscle. He was too big. Everything about him was over-sized—his eyes were rounded, his nose was on the overly-large size, and his wide mouth revealed a cluster of white teeth—but somehow it all worked to form one big baby face. I wondered if he even shaved, and knew right away this one was a teddy bear…or a Labrador.

"Good lord. Are you descended of bears or something?"

The words just rolled out of my mouth before I even considered whether they might be offensive or not. I had yet to be schooled on the subtleties and nuances of this strange new world, but realized questioning a person's origins might not be politically correct. I resolved—again—to work on my brain-to-mouth filter.

"Oh, god. I'm sorry. I…"

Luckily, he took pity on me and interrupted with a wicked grin.

"Don't sweat it. All you need to know is that I'm all man."

I think it took everything he had not to adjust himself to illustrate the point. And I swear his nostrils flared.

"Forgive our horn-dog friend. His humanoid sense of smell is so limited that he sniffs up every skirt on the rare occasion he gets lucky. I'm Layla. I've never met a real celebrity before. Will you sign my boobs?"

Layla, the funny one—I was guessing—was impersonating a Japanese anime character. Her long straight hair was black with bangs cut straight across her forehead. The thick locks were pulled back in a high ponytail except for two bright aqua strands hanging over her ears to fall on her shoulders.

At the boobs comment, she stretched open a white V-neck, revealing a tattoo that spanned her entire chest. A two-headed raven began at her collarbone and extended down into her slight cleavage. The intricate black outline of the tattoo was filled in with an aqua that matched the hue of her hair. The two ravens' heads stretched, open-mouthed, toward her shoulders as if cawing before taking flight upon a pair of outstretched wings.

The bird's tail wasn't fully visible, but I could just glimpse the top of two powerful talons gathered high into its body. Layla's slight frame topped out just over five feet, but five-inch platform boots that hugged her legs all the way up her reedy thighs put her nearly at my eye level. A tightly-fitted black leather jacket with tiny daggers for buttons completed her Miniature Badass ensemble.

"Can it, crow," the big man retorted. "And put the girls away. Everyone here has already seen 'em, anyway."

Layla wasn't fazed by the banter and dramatically rolled her eyes at the big guy, who surged forward with his hand out.

"Name's Boone Adder. This is Bex, and that's Ewan." He nodded in the direction of the other two, who both nodded at me in turn.

Bex very obviously had feline forbearers. She exuded sleek and haughty. Her long silky hair was a rich caramel color, her skin tone only a shade lighter. Her eyes, the color of honey, were wide and bright in the middle, but slanted sharply at both corners. I imagined her circling her prey, ass in the air and tail switching, though no tail was presently visible. She was attractive, sexy—the kind of girl that always seemed to attract older men and had no time for 'boys.'

Ewan, though, looked to be as homo sapien as I was.

Growing up in the South, I hadn't seen many men with overly-long hair. I'd known one or two who expressed their pride of heritage with traditional long locks, and there had been shag-cut trends, but by and large most men I knew kept their hair cropped close to their scalp. This guy, though, had the most gorgeous head of hair I had seen on a man. Shiny black curls fell in layers almost to the top of his shoulders in back, and just around his temples in the front. No hair was in its proper place, but it was perfect just the same. He rocked the look, no doubt about it.

Big, dark-brown eyes with almost curly black lashes studied my face. The slender slope of his nose peaked, skimmed over slight nostrils and into cheeks that looked downy soft compared to the perpetual five o'clock shadow that ran the length of his jawbone and into splashing of sideburns. A hint of a mustache brought attention to his mouth, which flashed bright white teeth for just a moment as he smiled warmly in welcome.

"Stella enrolled today. She's my new suitemate," announced Timbra.

Everyone offered congratulations. Well, most everyone. Bex's top lip twitched, though she covered it quickly. I wasn't sure if it was my new status as a student that she objected to, or that I was Timbra's suitemate. Ultimately, I decided that she saw me as competition. Cats.

"Aw, that's my jam," threw in the big man. "Stella, care to dance?"

I did. The bass was thumping, the dance floor was packed, and I had never been opposed to fun. I shot Timbra a wide-eyed smile and made my way to the middle of the room. Boone followed, and I was soon shaking my ass like there was church tomorrow.

Boone had good moves for someone so large. I figured him a humper for sure, but he surprised me with polite distance and fun spins and dips. We returned to the group when the next song turned out to be a ballad.

From the corner of my eye, I spotted Gresham near the bar. I excused myself and made my way over. He saw me and raised his head in recognition.

"I thought you weren't coming."

"Change of plans," he replied.

He looked fantastic, and I couldn't tell if he had tried to, or if it was something hastily thrown together. A tan blazer topped a sapphire V-neck T-shirt. Dark denim jeans ran into worn brown leather loafers with no socks.

"You seem to be getting along fine," he said. "You've made friends already, I see. I know the Redfern girl's family. Don't recognize the others."

"Yes, I think they're all freshmen, like me, so you wouldn't have had them in class yet."

"Primos, not freshmen. But I don't teach here. Is that what you thought? That I'm a professor?" He seemed to find this immensely humorous and his eyes twinkled. "Here," he said. "Your necklace has turned." His big hands were warm on my collarbone as he adjusted my pendant. A jolt of electricity shot from my neck, straight through the center of my body, and all the way to my toes. I shivered and his smile widened. Then darkened.

"Well...ah...yes," I stammered. " I mean...of course, now that I think about it, it would be weird that a professor crossed worlds and sought out a potential student. But, if you're not a teacher here, what do you do?"

"I do...special projects."

"Special projects like crashing SUV's into innocent girls, destroying their personal property, forcibly removing them from the scene of an accident, breaking into their apartment, and very nearly sexually assaulting them?"

"Now, hold on. I did not break into your apartment. And I apologized about my...physical response, though don't expect me to apologize again. Furthermore, I saved you from burning alive in that car, and for the last time—you hit me."

"Where did you get those cars, anyway, Mr. Gresham? And why does someone from a world where money is an afterthought choose SUVs and sports cars instead of something usefully utilitarian like, say, a Taurus?"

"A Taurus?" he snarled and scraped his tongue between his teeth, as if removing a bad taste from his mouth. "I rented those cars. I like nice things."

"Mmm-hmmm," I hummed playfully. Boy, riling him up was just too easy. Was I flirting? Maybe.

My attempt to hide my grin behind a sip of my drink was unsuccessful, and the tension soon left his shoulders. As I inquired further about Gresham's "special projects," I caught sight of a lovely brunette in her late thirties as she approached him from behind. She ran her hand through Gresham's arm and clasped his bicep possessively.

"Hello," she said coolly. "I'm Livia Miles."

She pronounced this la-VEE-yah. Her gray eyes were sharp and assessing as she took in my proximity to Gresham. I backed up a step instinctively. She extended a bony hand, and I took the time to do a little assessing of my own. Now, I like to consider myself fairly well-groomed, but Livia was the type of woman who always looked…pristine. Her nails were perfectly manicured, and the shine on her toe polish caused me to blink. Her smooth skin had obviously been exfoliated and buffed to perfection, her makeup was flawless, if on the heavy side. Her jewelry was tasteful and expensive, and her hair…god, her long brown curls absolutely gleamed reflecting the overhead lights. A tight black lace dress revealed a runner's legs and no breasts to speak of, thank the good lord for small mercies.

"Livia, this is Stella Stonewall," Gresham put in. "Stella is a primos, and will likely be in your department's Intro to Craft and Ritual class."

"I know who she is, Gresham," she said icily.

"Oh, uhm… Nice to meet you, Professor Miles," I stumbled. "Craft? I'm sorry; Orientation is tomorrow. I know very little about the coursework here."

"Dean Miles," she corrected. "Craft. The art and science of causing change in accordance with one's will."

I must have looked as clueless as I felt, because she turned to Gresham.

"Ugh. Rowan. She is an imbecile. Wherever did you find her, and what moron allowed her into this institution? If this is the caliber of student my department is expected to instruct, I…"

"Stella is new to our ways, as you know, Livia," Gresham growled. "She is a bright young woman, and will catch on quickly, I am sure, with the help of exceptional teachers like you."

To this obvious schmoozing, Livia seemed appeased. I had a sneaking suspicion he had just saved me from some serious in-class discrimination.

I couldn't recall the last time I had been so flagrantly insulted. Fifteen responses and backhanded insults raced through my mind, as did a speedy synopsis of my circumstances—new town, new school, new teacher. Don't make enemies, I told myself. Swallow your pride. Hold your tongue.

But the fact was I had real difficulty with those particular virtues.

"I look forward to learning as much as I can from someone with so many years of experience behind them," I said, perhaps a tad tartly. "My best days are still ahead of me, you know, and I could use a mentor."

Her eyes flashed with loathing at my implied slight to her age. Guess I hit a sore spot.

Gresham wheezed deep in his throat before recovering himself, though his eyes still shone with repressed laughter as he bid me goodnight and led her to the bar.

"Stella, it is time to wake. It is Thursday, May thirteenth. The time now is seven a.m."
"Stella, it is time to wake. It is Thursday, May thirteenth. The time now is seven a.m."

I opened one eye to the rude and monotonous awakening. I knew that voice. Pia.

Just before I fell asleep the night before, I lay back on the worn quilt with my hands behind my head, recalling the dizzying amount of new information I had gained. After a while, I noticed tiny scribbles all over the cracked plaster ceiling. I stood on the bed to get a better look and found the ceiling was covered with signatures—I assumed those of the previous occupants. Some were tight, rigid forms of letters; others slanting and flourished. All were a dark burnt-umber color. The thought of those who had lain in my bed, lived and studied in that very room, was bizarre and deeply intriguing. How many years had Radix students been occupying my room? A hundred years, certainly. Five hundred? More?

I had fallen asleep contemplating the history the school possessed, and dreamed of women dressed in hip pads, corsets, and full skirts. I dreamed of men with plaited hair and longswords, and in that real but apparitional way of dreams,

61

two familiar faces appeared among the costumed crowd. A stunning brunette possessively clasped the upper arm of a powerfully built man with an unruly mane of black hair and piercing amber eyes.

"Morning, Pia," I mumbled, one side of my face still firmly planted in a pillow.

"Good morning, Stella. The time now is seven-oh-one a.m. The Radix Primo Anno Orientation begins in fifty-nine minutes. You are required to attend this function that is expected to break for a one-hour lunch at noon and conclude by four p.m."

"Wait. Ano what? And would it be so hard to wake me with a little energizing music? Some encouragement, maybe, or at least some sort of pleasantry? This 'The time now' business is so...sterile. I'm a morning person; let's start the day off right."

"Pleasant?" Pia asked. "Encouraging? I'm sorry, Stella. I must have missed the memo that your mother was also enrolling in The Root."

"Humor. Now that's more like it, Pia."

I jumped in the shower and hurriedly dressed for the day. I had brought my favorite jeans—the ones I knew made my butt look good. One less thing to worry about. Timbra was nowhere to be seen, so I headed downstairs for coffee.

"JEEN-jah! Pleasant morning? Coffee?"

It was Knox, the frustratingly adorable bartender/barista.

"My. Name. Is. Stella. Aren't you chipper this morning? I'll take a..."

"Let me guess. Hmmm. Mocha. Nonfat. Covered with whipped cream."

"That's exactly right. How did you know?" I supposed he could add mind reader to his growing list of useful talents.

"A lucky guess. Would you settle for vanilla, though? The nonfat and whipped cream I have covered, but even this tan would never qualify as 'mocha'."

This he said with an easy smile, and I laughed, despite myself.

"Are you headed to the big orientation today, then?"

"Yes. I'm in desperate need of a crash course. I have a lot to learn, and I already feel the disadvantage. I've made some friends, and their parents are alumni, as were their grandparents and great-grandparents—their connections to this place go back hundreds of years. They've always known they would go here; they're prepared for it. I'm afraid I'll stick out like a sore thumb."

"Oh, don't fear that, Ginger. You do stick out, I'll tell ye now."

I groaned in despair, but he went on, "No, no. Think of your ignorance as a gift. You're new, you're fresh, you're a blank slate. You have nothing to prove, no familial expectations, no one to impress or let down. Absorb everything like a sponge, and enjoy it. There's a whole new world out there; dive right in."

The truth in his blunt assessment made me feel better, as did the encouragement. I left with a latte and a croissant in hand and a smile on my face.

"A nonfat mocha latte has 220 calories and three grams of fat."

This unwelcome commentary came from my personal interactive assistant.

"Oh, hell no, Pia. You turn that function off right now."

"Just trying to be helpful."

"So not helpful. You want to help? Where am I going for this orientation?"

"I'm more than a map, you know," Pia mumbled.

* * *

I entered Martyrskirk Theatre and scanned those seated until I spotted Timbra. She held up a hand, and I took the seat that she'd saved. I spotted Ewan and Layla and some others in the surrounding seats and smiled.

"Good morning, and welcome to you, the 921st entering Primos Class of Radix Citadel for Supernatural Learning," a stern, confident female voice boomed through the theater.

"I'm Faye Edgecliffe, vice chancellor of this esteemed institution, and it is my pleasure to tell you that for nearly a millennium Radix has maintained a reputation as Thayer's leading center for magical instruction and research. The institution has provided an invigorating intellectual and introspective climate in which our graduates have learned to harness their full potential as individuals, benefiting themselves, their families, and society as a whole."

"Gods, how long will she blather on, you think?"

This from Timbra, who I was shocked to hear utter a disparaging remark. She looked lovely and casual in a black top, thin heather gray leggings and black flats. Her almond-colored hair hung loosely about her shoulders. I shook my head, wide-eyed not because I didn't know, but because *I did not know* the history and prominence behind the school in which I was now enrolled.

Vice Chancellor Edgecliffe continued, "This year, Radix received sixteen applications per availability. Having met our standards and been chosen, you know too well that Radix sets highly challenging entrance requirements to attract only the most academically and magically potent students in the arts, sciences, and physical forms of the supernatural. Our reputation for delivering the highest quality instruction and research makes Radix the most sought after institution the world over."

The Vice Chancellor continued on about the superiority and exclusivity of Radix, but I heard nothing else. All thought centered on her claims that the school received 16 applications per spot available, and that the entrance requirements were steep.

Was this true? How in the world had I gained a spot, considering I was an unknown, last minute applicant? Actually, I hadn't even applied. I had just shown up and enrolled. I had a bad feeling about it. I was smart enough to know that when something seemed too good to be true, it usually was.

I came out of my reverie to a hard elbow to the arm.

"Ow. What'd you do that for?"

"Look, it's your friend from the mixer." Timbra nodded at the stage. "RBF has taken the stage."

I had told her about my encounter with Dean Miles. We had both decided that, while strikingly beautiful, Livia Miles definitely suffered from 'Resting Bitch Face.'

I snorted, but quickly gained my composure when I saw her. RBF was in full effect, all right, as she strode confidently to the mic. A high bun made her look more severe, but no less lovely. A copper-colored academic gown with gold embellishments draped her artfully as the hem met sleek, tan, muscular calves. Her very high-heeled gold pumps clack, clack, clacked as she took her place behind the podium.

"Hello, students. Your acceptance to this institution marks the beginning of your personal journey, not just into the physical world of your own genetic lineage, but into the metaphysical worlds of magic and the supernatural. As Dean of the Department of Craft and Ritual, it is my honor to give you an overview of today's orientation. A successful Radix student will learn to strike a balance between academic and practical coursework. Please refer to your prospectus as I outline the departments that comprise Radix, Citadel for Supernatural Learning."

I opened a thin booklet and flipped through the first few pages.

Department Of Botany
History of Herbalism; ID'ing Our Herbal Allies: Medicinal or Magical?; Practical Preparation and Application

Department Of Craft And Ritual
Intro to Craft and Ritual, Advanced C& R, Magical Myths and Legends, The Chemistry of Craft, Magical Methods: Manifesting Change; Tools of the Trade: Charms, Talismans and Amulets

Department Of Divinity
The 4 G's: Ghosts, Guides, Guardians and Gods; Duality and Polarity; Deities; Omens and Prophesy; Runic Divination

Center For Magical Law And Ethics
The Ethics of Spellcrafting; Professional Responsibility; Who's Your Daddy: Libel and Slander

Department Of Modern And Medieval Languages
Latin; History of Spellcrafting; Advanced Telepathy

Center For Physical Form
Finding Your Metamorphosis; Advanced Control; Metamorphosis lab

Center For Psychic Development
Breaking Bad: Psychic Self Defense; Meditation and Consciousness

Center For Thayerian Studies
Evolutionary and Supernatural Historical Study; Cultural Anthropology of Thayer; Historical Importance of Thayerian Fae; Gnomenculture

A

The remainder of the day was filled with tours of the sprawling campus, team building exercises, and firm reminders of the standard to which Radix students were held. The day flew by, and in no time at all it was four p.m.

Pia was beside herself to inform me that a group dinner was scheduled that evening in the large banquet hall. After a quick change into an airy summer dress I headed for the banquet hall, thankful I'd had the foresight to pack several different outfits.

Timbra and I entered the massive gray rubble masonry building that said 'Crusades' much more than it said 'college.' I thought it must have been a medieval banquet hall because two towering wood doors with iron bolts like fists and hinges the length of my forearm opened into cavernous room that could hold at least 600 people. The stone floors were uneven, though they had supported so many footfalls that the edges were smooth and nearly shiny.

Long, worn wooden tables and benches, now gray and porous with age, formed rows the width of the room and stopped within feet of a large dais. The platform held three more tables, these with ancient wooden chairs and decorated with ornate candelabras and tasteful muted arrangements.

Faded tapestries depicting ancient battle scenes covered most of the walls of the hall; these artfully framed by medieval weaponry. Swords, bows, maces, mauls, and bludgeoning devices of all sorts gave the drafty dining room a welcoming touch. Despite the overwhelming impression of frost, death, and dank, a glorious smell of roasted meat, onions, and butter wafted throughout the hall.

"What's with this place?" I asked Timbra once we had found a place to sit among the worn benches. "Are they going to feed us gruel and salted herring? Though, if that's the case, bring on the mead. I had some once at a beekeeper's wedding. Nom, nom. That stuff is dan-ger-ous."

"Well, I'm a vegetarian, so let's hope they don't send out a whole roasted pig."

"Oh, I never thought of that. I suppose being descended of deer you wouldn't eat meat."

"No, I don't."

"Is a person's ancestry an okay topic to ask about? This is all so new to me," I said apologetically. "I don't want to offend anyone, but I have a million questions."

"In general, it is a perfectly fine topic of discussion. Some people are more or less proud of their lineage than others. Bex, you might have noticed, is exceedingly fond of her descent from lions."

"Yes, I had. She holds her nose so high I thought if it rained she might drown."

Timbra guffawed at the precise moment Bex and the others took seats at our table.

"What's funny?" This from Layla, who'd today coordinated her teal hair and prominent tattoo with an orange tank and a short, tight jean skirt.

Timbra, though warming up to me, was still quite shy in a group. It was fascinating to observe the change in her. One-on-one she was fun, interesting, but as more people joined her sphere of interaction, the more reserved she became.

"Stella wants to learn to make mead," she blurted.

This only served to confuse the newcomers, since it wasn't the least bit funny, but I appreciated the solidarity and smiled warmly at her in acknowledgment.

The majority of primos students had found seats, and before long a wait staff brought out glasses of water and a salad course.

"Does anyone know the history of this banquet hall?" I asked. "It's so odd they're serving us here. I really think they're feeding us on the same table they used for butchering. There has to be a more suitable place for our class size."

"Not to mention more appetizing locales without blood-caked weapons as decor," threw in Ewan, who until then I had not heard utter a single word. His resonant voice held humor that I hadn't expected; he always looked so brooding and serious.

I caught his deep brown eyes as I grinned, and he held my attention for several beats. I hadn't noticed it before, but the chemistry between us was unmistakable. Afraid that the others at the table had noticed our moment, I dragged my eyes away and concentrated on my salad. As I took a bite, I dared a glance in Ewan's direction again. Those intelligent eyes still followed me, though now they betrayed a deeper interest. It was mutual.

"…father told me about this place," Boone continued, nudging me back into the present. "He said it's customary for primos to dine in the banquet hall as a reminder of the gravity of our circumstances. He said that sure, there's a lot of fun to be had and memories to be made in our time here, but we must never forget Thayer's important and sometimes tragic history. And we must remember the reason we're here is to discover our true powers and our value as citizens and protectors of Thayer."

It wasn't Boone's big frame alone that commanded attention; he had that 'something' that born leaders posses—an ability to compel those around them not just to listen, but to look to them for answers. And he was really a gifted storyteller. I barely knew him, but I trusted him already.

"Your father seems like a smart man," Timbra gushed softly.

"He is. He taught me everything I know. Very little of it has useful application," he said with an easy grin.

"He coulda taught your big ass some manners," Layla teased. "Here, wipe that drool off your face."

Boone shot Layla the finger, but also shot a covert glance in Timbra's direction.

Ahhh. The big man shows his cards, I thought.

The main course, a delicious roast Cornish hen—in fact, not a pig—was served much to Timbra's chagrin, though she was a super sport about it. Bex had been markedly silent

throughout dinner, busily tapping away on her P.I.A which, I
learned, she had named 'Bexy.'

"It's no coincidence that rhymes with 'sexy,'" she loftily
informed us.

I wondered if she had thought that through—the
implication of course that 'Bex' rhymed with 'sex.' Probably.

After finishing her meal, she announced her departure and
swish, swished her curvy ass all the way out of the hall.

The remaining five of our little group enjoyed an elegant
dessert surrounded by our new classmates. We left the
medieval hall in good spirits but with a firm grasp of the
intended significance of our situations. Our attendance at
Radix was more than fun times and self-discovery. We were
there to learn to protect ourselves, our families, and our
communities from very real threats.

A

It was at this point that I wondered how I was going to get
back home.

I hadn't seen nor heard from Gresham since he left the
mixer with Livia, whom I inferred from the possessive pawing
was his…girlfriend? I was more than a little disappointed at
that thought, though I wasn't sure why. It was true that
something about his darkly mysterious persona scared me
senseless. And he was certainly very grumpy. And too old for
me.

But, oh, there was just something about him that set my
blood on fire. He may have whispered danger, but he screamed
virility. Maybe it was some deep-seeded female need to win the
Alpha Male, which he certainly was. My, oh my, was he.

Ahem. Tongue back in your mouth, Stella.

At any rate, I didn't have a number for him or have the
slightest idea where to find him. We had planned to return
home after Radix Orientation; my roommate Lizzie was
certainly expecting me.

As I walked across campus with the group, talking and laughing, I recognized Gresham's rigid stance as we approached Sabre Hall.

"Stella, I value my time and expect you to do the same. I do not appreciate being kept waiting," he barked.

Timbra and the others cut questioning eyes at me as they meekly scooted past. I wished they had stayed around, because I planned to give Gresham a strongly-worded inquisition on just who the hell he thought he was, talking to me that way. But they did leave. Cowards.

"Waiting?" I asked. "I haven't heard from you since you left with RBF last night. How was I supposed to know you were waiting out here?"

"I left a message with your Pia. Didn't you get it? And what is RBF?"

"Pia? Oh hell. I turned her off because she kept prattling on about the fat grams in ganache," I waved Pia's nonsense away with a flick of the wrist.

"RBF is Livia. Stands for Resting Bitch Face."

I had heard it only once before, and can only compare Gresham's roar of laughter to an amusement park ride. What at first sent a jolt of fear through me by its intensity suddenly morphed into something evoking a pure and thrilling joy, leaving me lightheaded and breathless.

A

After a run upstairs and a quick goodbye to Timbra, who made me pinkie promise to return, I grabbed my overnight bag and met Gresham in the courtyard. Still grinning with mirth, he laced his hand with mine, shocking me again.

"Hold on, Stella. I'm taking you home. You remember how?"

I nodded, lifted a foot, and together we stepped through the unfathomable, invisible barrier between my world and his.

With my impending move, Friday morning seemed an excellent time to serve my current roommate and BFF one last big breakfast. While she slept some of the party off from the night before and dreamed of elusive glasses of cool, clear water, I whipped up real bacon, drop biscuits, and creamy chocolate gravy made of five essential ingredients—butter, sugar, flour, milk, and cocoa.

The moment I pressed 'brew' on the coffee pot Lizzie managed to lumber into the kitchen.

"You didn't miss much last night," she said.

"No? Nobody passed out in the ladies? No scandalous hookups?"

"Huh-uh. Tonight, though, everybody's going to be out. We're going."

"Oh, I don't know. I have a lot to do. I need to pack," I said, and then cringed in regret. I had a plan to break my news smoothly.

Lizzie's eyebrows wadded up in confusion. I could almost hear her brain thinking. It took a while, but she finally concluded she had no idea what I was packing for.

The preceding night Gresham had deposited me at the front door of my apartment building. We said short goodbyes and he promised to return to help with my move to Radix. In that way an unconscious mind can collate and process information without the impedance of a cognizance, sleep provided me with several indisputable facts. I had written them down.

1) My mom had been actively keeping a much bigger secret from me than I could ever have suspected.
2) My "father" was from another world. Plain and simple.
3) He was probably out there somewhere.
4) I needed to inform everyone I was leaving town.
5) I needed to come up with a really good lie.
6) I needed to pack.

I had come up with what I considered a really great lie while frying bacon.

Before she could ask I jumped right in. "Lizzie, I have some news. It's a once in a lifetime opportunity. Really exciting. I hope you'll be happy for me."

She perked up right away. "Well, what is it?"

"I've been accepted into an exclusive astronomy fellowship in South Africa."

"South Africa?" she breathed.

"Mmm. Hmm. I was an alternate. Someone dropped out at the last minute and I have to pack up and leave right away."

"Oh," she said, not thrilled at all, before catching herself and putting on an enthusiastic front for my behalf. "That's wonderful. I'm so proud of you."

"Thank you, sweetie," I forced out. Guilt nearly compelled me to tell the truth as she hugged me in congratulations.

"I just...I just didn't know you'd applied to anything like that. I thought we'd be roommates for a while longer," Lizzie said. "How long will you be gone?"

"Oh, it's a year-long fellowship, and then there will be an opportunity to extend or transfer. I'm afraid I don't know when I could be back. I'll pay rent through next month so you have time to find somebody."

"I'm not worried about that, Stell. This is just so sudden. I thought we had forever."

"I did too. But I have to go. This isn't something I can turn down." My stomach twisted at the thought of leaving Lizzie, of lying to her, but I had to maintain the facade. I could hardly say I had enrolled in an academy for supernatural beings in an alternate world, had a mysterious magical daddy, and an awesome new suite-mate whose ears protruded four inches from her head.

No. Lie I must, and lie I would, as awful as it made me feel.

Lizzie offered to help me pack, and made me promise to go out with her that night. One last hurrah.

The rest of the day was spent reminiscing our years together and wishing we were still as skinny as the day we set foot on campus. We finished packing my things that afternoon.

I was feeling and looking good as we entered Maxine's. I had opted for my special-occasion slinky top with tiny stones that sparkled like onyx stars as I danced...which I did. A lot.

Lizzie was right, everyone was out. I said goodbye to those I had come to know and love. For a few hours, I compartmentalized all the new things waiting for me in Thayer and said goodbye to college life, and the last four years.

A

A mallet-wielding mammoth battered at my brain. Repeatedly. Why did I have those last two beers?

That was the thing about drinking, though. You drank to get buzzed, and then failed to realize when you reached that critical point, passing it up entirely and entering a new state I like to call "shitballs." Blitzed, befuggered, Amy Winehoused— too soon?—there are a thousand ways to say it, and they all end with one thing in common—a massive friggin' headache.

I had one, and the person pounding on my door was sure to make it worse.

"Morning, Mom." I was certain I looked as hellish as I felt. If my mother said nine, she would barely wait for eight-fifteen, I swear to god.

"Happy graduation day, baby."

My mom was a perfect example of someone suffering from 'selective comprehension.' I'm sure she knew I had been out all night and was hungover, but she chose to ignore the entire situation and go on as if nothing was amiss. She abhorred confrontation, and would avoid it at all costs. I am convinced the reason I'm such an assertive asshole is because my whole life I watched her allow everyone she encountered to walk all over her. It was sad, really, to think how someone could get to that point, to wonder what could have happened in her early life to turn her into this pliant, meek, fragment of a person.

But, my mother had the kindest, purest heart I had ever encountered and an unending, unconditional love for me. I loved her immensely.

"I brought breakfast sandwiches," she said, "and coffee. Here, you go take a shower while I warm these sandwiches up. My baby's college graduation is in less than two hours. Yay!"

A

At ten a.m. in the school's multi-purpose arena, I stood in several lines, listened for my name, crossed the stage, shook the dean's hand, waved to my mom, and found my place in yet another line. Graduation was nothing short of anti-climatic. But, I did it, and it made my mom happy.

Upon hearing the news of my "fellowship," my mother was ecstatic, encouraging, and bursting with pride. I felt like a real dick for lying to her, but my every instinct screamed not to tell her the truth. She was so delicate, and was obviously hiding something from me about that side of my life. No, I would pursue my new life in Thayer on my own for now.

I had planned to confront my mother about my father again—in person this time—at lunch so she couldn't hang up the phone or run from the room plugging her ears and screaming '*nah, nah, nah, nah, nah*' but she invited Lizzie and her family to join us, so the conversation never happened. I resolved to get her alone that afternoon under the guise of a little shopping, but shortly after lunch she announced that she needed to rush back home.

I followed her to her car; I would chase her if I had to in order to get the information I needed. When she attempted to hug me goodbye, I grabbed her by both arms, moving my head around to follow her face until she looked me in the eyes.

"Mom?" I pleaded, my gaze darting between hers, imploring her for an answer. "Mom, please tell me what you know about my father. It's important. Some things have come up and I…I need answers."

She searched my gaze only briefly then studied the ground. Her little lip trembled and she dashed tears from the corners of her crinkled eyes.

"Stella, I can't. Please don't ask me to do this. I just…I just can't."

Her petite frame wracked as a sob escaped before she could wrench it back in.

"I'll pray for you," she whispered, and squeezed my hands. "You and I may not have all the answers, but God does. Goodbye, sweetie."

She drove away to the safety of her own home, leaving me neither with answers, nor the knowledge of where I might find them.

I kicked absently at something on the sidewalk bordering our dingy student apartments. There was no breeze on the May afternoon, and the stale air was dense and oppressive as I tried to understand my mother's motivations. I feared I never would. I looked to the sky for answers, but it only mocked me, blinding me as if the heavens, too, wanted to change the subject.

Defeated, I turned to head back inside.

I ran firmly into the steely chest of Rowan Gresham.

*T*he reality was that I didn't own much, which made me feel a little better about the move. On some level I always resisted putting down roots. At least I could turn my indecisiveness into a positive, and take the next step in my progressively weird life.

Once the clothes I liked enough to take were packed, I was left with a very large donation box and a few pieces of hand-me-down furniture, which I gifted once more to Lizzie. I took some photos, a few beloved books, a favorite blanket, and that was it.

Gresham grabbed a large suitcase with one big hand, and balanced a lidded bank box with the opposing arm. I slung a large duffel bag full of shoes over my shoulder and grabbed another big suitcase. We stood alone in my living room loaded and ready when I realized that both of our hands were full; I couldn't connect to him to warp to Thayer.

He looked to me encouragingly.

"You can do this, Stella. We'll travel together. Simply picture Sabre's Grand Hall. I will, too, and we'll reunite there."

I could only nod my willingness to try, my windpipe suddenly clogged with anxiety, but then I cleared my throat and stood up straight.

"All right. Let's do this."

I lifted one foot, imagined one of the worn and supple leather club chairs I had seen the first time I entered Sabre Hall, and when I put my foot down...nothing happened.

For a split second I feared the worst, that I was stuck between two worlds and would never find my way out again.

A jolt rocked me from my doubt. My entire being was a bass guitar string stretched tight and unyielding, and someone had plucked me. Hard.

My eyes squinted of their own volition, my teeth chattered, and the core of my body reverberated, bouncing around within a hollow chamber. When the reverberation slowed, though, and I could open my eyes, I found I was standing beside the leather chair.

I was so happy I let out a proud "Yee-yah!" and looked around for Gresham. He stood just a few feet away at the bottom of the stairs.

I must have looked as jarred as I felt because he smiled and nodded encouragingly.

"Don't worry. It gets easier with practice. It won't always feel as though you've gone through a meat grinder."

A

"Next time we travel with luggage, Gresham, I wish you would recommend that we aim for my bedroom, and skip the stairs. Hmmm? This is work."

The duffel of shoes was heavy because, hey, a girl needs a lot of shoes. Lugging it and the suitcase up four flights of stairs seemed incredibly dumb when the whole ordeal could have been avoided. Warping into Thayer zapped a large chunk of my energy, and I was really struggling.

"Well, I've not been in your bedroom, so it is hard for me to imagine it," he replied coolly while ascending the stairs with ease.

"Besides," he said, his mood suddenly darker, "I don't consider the effort spent before one gets to the bedroom to be 'work.' That's the good part."

Wait, whah? Was that innuendo? From Mr. You're-Too-Young?

I couldn't see his face since he was a few stairs ahead of me. I was stunned and had unwittingly stopped climbing. Gresham turned around to face me, those amber eyes shining with amusement.

"What? Have I scandalized you again?"

His wolfish smile gave nothing away. Predator or prankster I couldn't be sure.

I decided to go on the offensive.

"Not scandalized. I'm just shocked. I mean, what would Livia think about you practically propositioning innocent young college girls?"

I gave my best impression of an innocent young college girl and blinked wide virginal eyes at him.

"Oh, I can see right through you, and an innocent you certainly are not. That said, The Root is a training ground for adults. You had better be on guard with a bod...er...well, be on your guard."

It didn't escape my notice that he had not addressed the mention of Livia, but I decided to change tracks.

"Speaking of being on my guard, Gresham, why are you helping me?"

I grunted, dragging the two bags behind me as I struggled up each stair.

"Why did you come find me?"

Step.

"For that matter, how did you even know I existed?"

Step.

"And while we're at it, how did I get into this prestigious school?"

I had stopped climbing, exhausted and ready for some answers.

Gresham turned, but not to look at me. He faced the door to my new home.

"Ah. Here we are. 412."

"I want answers, Gresham. I've been thrown into this new world, leaving behind every friend and family member I ever had. I think I've been damned pliable throughout this whole ordeal, but I have questions and I deserve answers."

I was working my way up to a fit.

"Not in the hallway, Stella. I'll answer what questions I can, I swear it, but not here, not now. For today, just enjoy your new home and your new friends."

Timbra had heard my rising voice and stuck her head into the hall. Her cervid ears twitched with curiosity even as she smiled hello.

"I think you can take it from here," Gresham said. "Another project requires I be out of town for the next few days. I wish you luck in your first week of courses."

With that abrupt announcement, he turned and strode back down the stairs, brokering no further conversation.

"What exactly is his role?" Timbra was no dummy. "I know you're new to Thayer and all, but he seems an awfully menacing babysitter. He helped you move? And is it just me or is he scalding hot for an old guy?"

I nodded reluctantly.

"No one back home knows I'm here. I think he feels he owes me because he's the reason I'm here alone. He found me and introduced me to Thayer, to The Root. To be honest, I still have a lot of questions, but I'm starting to think he's intentionally avoiding them."

"Well, you're wrong about one thing. You're not alone." She smiled warmly. "Here, let me help you inside."

*O*n the first day of class I was both thrumming with excitement and nauseous with apprehension. Add to those states of mind a double shot chai latte from my favorite in-house cafe, and the result can best be described as "punchy."

Luckily, most primos had the same course schedule, and my new BFF Timbra was there to guide my twitchy ass across campus to our very first class, Intro to Craft and Ritual. We took seats near the front of the large theater-style classroom that easily held most of our entering class's one hundred students. I spotted Layla, Boone, and Ewan on the way down to our seats and waved hello.

"Who's that?" I asked Timbra, nodding to a serious-looking guy talking with Ewan before class began.

"Raynor McKellan. From up North. Descended of seals."

His dark skin was a beautiful deep gray or granite color and seemed somehow denser than most; so thick it was almost shiny. Each time he turned his head, his skin picked up light and vacillated between black, silver, gray and even a lovely espresso. Sleek black hair stood straight up before falling back onto his scalp like dense fur.

Noticing his hair was just an afterthought because Raynor's powerful face stole any attention placed elsewhere. Regal. He was regal without effort. His strong jaw was set in a square. Mesmerizing clear gray eyes glared from beneath slender arched brows. The severe gaze was almost luminescent, and when it swung in my direction, I immediately looked away before he read my every secret.

A choked, "Intense," was all I could manage.

"Very," agreed Timbra. "He's actually quite…"

Movement at the front of the classroom directed our attention elsewhere and hushed conversations. The professor entering through a door at the side of the dais was not one I expected, and I extracted my syllabus to be sure. No, I was right; the syllabus listed Sid Cromwell as leading the Intro to Craft class. I really thought I had dodged a bullet not having Dean Miles this year.

Please, oh please, don't let her be the professor. I repeated this mantra over and over as she left the dais and advanced into the classroom until she stood in the center aisle midway up the bowl of seats. I wasn't certain if making people uncomfortable came naturally to her, or if she had to work at it. But whatever the effort, the result was the same; she was intimidating as hell. She addressed the class abruptly in her crisp, resonant voice.

"Professor Cromwell has withdrawn from the university at short notice, leaving me inadequate time to find a replacement. Consequently, I will be instructing your Intro to Craft and Ritual class until further notice. I hope you grasp the merit of this circumstance; I have not taught this class in some years. Some of the information I will cover will likely be difficult for some of you to grasp." Here I swear she looked pointedly in my direction. "But I cannot be expected to dumb down curriculum or hold any hands. Either keep up, or go back home."

"I really think we need to add ABF to her list of nicknames," whispered Timbra through one side of her mouth, while keeping her gaze trained on Dean Miles.

To my questioning, "Hmm?" she added, "Active. As in, active bitch face, as well as resting."

I couldn't contain the snort of laughter, and knew I was in trouble the moment it escaped. Dean Miles' head whipped back in my direction and her severely gorgeous face took on a look of evil pleasure.

Damn. I bet she cracks a mean whip in the bedroom.

That thought brought with it unwelcome images of her muscled legs sheathed in dominatrix boots and straddling Gresham as she ran the thong of a bullwhip across his straining pectoral. Even more unwelcome was the knot of unbridled jealousy that made me want to grab a hank of her chestnut hair and slap the bitch right off her face.

Wherethehelldidthatcomefrom?

"…Miss Stonewall? Are you still with us? Have you confused my class for Omens and Premonitions? I'll ask you to keep your consciousness in the here and now, if you please."

My gaze, admittedly still throwing green darts, snapped to Dean Miles' as I realized I had gone on another mental side trip.

"Oh, good," she smirked. "It looks like we have a volunteer."

Dean Miles instructed me to stand on the steps separating the two sides of the classroom. I knew her intent was to horrify me, but I resolutely refused to allow her to do it. I may have been new to her world, but I wasn't new to the game. I was born with a straight backbone, and she sure didn't have the stuff to break it.

Damned if she didn't try to bend it, though.

"Miss Stonewall, please tell the class the most important aspect of craft, spell casting, and magic in general."

When I didn't offer an answer she gleefully continued.

"Don't know? Hmm? Knowledge. Knowledge is the single most important aspect to utilizing the power that is inherent to us….well, to most of us."

She said this pointedly at me. Again. I really wasn't sure what I had done to garner such hostility. Surely she wasn't always so venomous. It was obvious I hadn't been called up to volunteer, but to serve as a punching bag.

"We must know the threats and the potential of the power around us; we must understand the tools, language, and rituals necessary to manipulate that power, and we must know ourselves. "Do you know who you are, Miss Stonewall? Do you know from where your innate magic comes? I daresay, *if* you posses any, you do not know how to use it or even the first place to look for it."

Now, I may be a redhead, but it really takes a lot to make me mad. Repeated intentional degradation in front of my peers will do the trick. I stood, seething and tight-fisted, my anger leashed only by my focus on the feel of fingernails digging into my palms.

"You may have heard the term 'chakra,' though it has many other names. Aura, third eye, essence, or energy. One's chakra is his or her access point to all of the power at their disposal."

At her mentions of chakra and third eye, I felt the familiar burning pressure in my chest that indicated I was having another panic attack.

Just great, Stonewall, I thought to myself. *Your fight or flight reflex is shit.*

But when next my heartbeat thumped, as it was known to do, rather than a fidgety panic, I was exhilarated and teeming with anticipation. I was a destrier fighting against a steel bit in an effort to join the battlefield. Without conscious effort, I lay my hand over my racing, thumping heart in wonder.

"Look," said a snide Dean Miles. " She does know something, doesn't she? Of course, one can have chakras in multiple locations; it varies from person to person." She nodded at me sarcastically, eyes wide in mocking approval. "That'll be all, Miss Stonewall. Take your seat."

God, I hated her. What I didn't understand was why she hated me.

As I stiffly sat back down, Timbra lay a sympathetic hand on my arm and shook her head in reassurance. I don't know what Dean Miles said the remainder of class; I tuned her out in favor of exploring my newfound chakra.

A

My schedule consisted of six classes and one lab, a heavy course load. Besides Intro to Craft and Ritual, I was enrolled in Cosmology 101, Finding Your Metamorphosis, Tools of the Trade, The Elements, History of Herbalism, and Breaking Bad: Psychic Self Defense.

I was happy to find my new friends shared my schedule. Timbra had a particular interest in the Herbalism class, though that was more a product of her predilection to eat herbs than to smoke them. A particularly bad hair day had me running behind schedule and I told Timbra to go ahead without me. After giving up and pulling my hair back into a high ponytail, I raced to Intro to Cosmology only to find the seat next to Timbra taken by Boone. She shrugged in apology and I sought seating elsewhere. Ewan raised his hand and indicated a free seat next to him.

The available seat was mid-row, and Ewan had to stand to let me pass. He was so big—both tall and broad—that even though I had turned sideways to face him, my breasts still inadvertently brushed his hard stomach. Though he tried to be discreet, I was certain that he made a deep, long intake of breath through his nose, not so much a gasp as sniffing me. Startled, I looked up at him. He didn't even have the good sense to be embarrassed.

His chocolate curls hung lazily around his brow and jawline, and his perpetual five o'clock shadow was in full effect. I held his gaze until he broke the connection, shamelessly raking my lips, my neck, and the tops of my breasts before boldly meeting my gaze again. He stood for what seemed like minutes just looking at me like…well, he looked at me like he wanted to devour me. I wasn't sure whether to be turned on or afraid. But when I realized I still stood within licking distance, crowding him at his chair rather than moving on to the next seat, I opted for embarrassed and sat down as quickly as I could.

Lost in my thoughts—about what I will not divulge—I failed to notice when the professor entered the classroom.

"Good morning, and welcome to Cosmology 101," boomed a deep voice that elicited visions of an Irish James Earl Jones. "I'm Aemon Lochlan."

I looked around the front of class for the professor, but couldn't see the speaker. I shot a questioning look at Ewan, who shrugged good naturedly and nodded toward the podium. I looked again, and then I saw him. It was the tiny professor that Gresham had brought to meet me at the coffee shop. I was thrilled to see him again. He looked just as stereotypically old world as I recalled. His tweed suit was in a blue herringbone pattern this time, with a matching blue sweater vest underneath. His thick white beard, while manicured, was long enough that it almost met a navy polka-dot bow tie. All that was missing was a pipe and a tattered copy of Walden.

He pushed horn-rimmed glasses up his nose authoritatively and continued, "I'll be your guide through this journey into Cosmology, which is defined as the study of the origin, evolution, and eventual fate of the universe…"

"Dum, dum, dummm…"

This from Ewan beside me. I grinned, and snuck a peek at him to see if I was still in danger of being eaten. The outlook was unclear, though he did seem to be trying to lighten the mood. He smiled at me charmingly. I know I must have given the wrong impression as I stared at him, moving my head from one side and then the other in deep contemplation of what his genetic makeup must be. He gave off a decidedly predatory vibe, but for the life of me I could not find any physical indicators of which predator.

Maybe he was just homo sapien, like me…no, not like me. I had no idea what secrets my elusive ancestry held. I was really looking forward to Finding Your Metamorphosis class.

For the remainder of Cosmology, though I faced forward, I could often feel Ewan's gaze. Tingles of warm attention caressed my neck, my cheeks, my collarbone, my eyes. I never faced him; I wasn't sure I could endure another soul-deep assessment and not reach out to him. I longed to touch him. I wanted to run my thumb along his dark brows, to pull one of his curls just to watch it spring back. That initial attraction I had noticed was no fluke, and the forcefulness of it was frightening.

I was unsure of my feelings about Ewan, unsure of the magnetic pull between us when I barely knew him. I did know one thing, though; getting involved with the wrong guy was not a good idea at this point in my life. I had some in-depth self discovery to conduct, and needed to avoid distraction. Without looking his way again I shot from my seat as soon as class dismissed and hotfooted it for the courtyard beyond the ancient double doors.

A

Timbra and I lunched at a lovely cafe along the river. The dishes were so complex and handcrafted with ripe fruit, roasted nuts, and other goodies that calling them 'salads' was a real injustice. Unfortunately, the Southern sweet tea phenomenon had not found its way to Thayer, but water was okay in a pinch.

Our next class, Finding Your Metamorphosis, was after lunch and I became more anxious of it with each passing moment.

"I'm nervous, too, Stella. That's normal." Timbra's confident air betrayed no nervousness whatsoever.

"Why would you be nervous?" I asked astonished. "You know what you turn into."

"I may know what, but I don't know how. I've never done it. I have the ears already, sure, but I've never taken my animal form. It's strictly forbidden until we learn the process at university, and even then only under the guidance of a mentor."

"Oh. Well. I guess I just thought maybe your parents had shown you; that it was something you grew up around."

"I have only seen my parents change a handful of times. Most only do it to hunt or fight and our family, you may have guessed, doesn't do much hunting. Very little fighting, apart from my raucous cousin Sadie and her sisters," she said with a grin.

"What's changing like? Is it violent? Messy? Scary?"

"No. From what I've seen it's just...natural. A normal part of life."

"If it's so normal, then I really don't understand why kids here aren't taught how to control their forms from childhood. It seems like you'd have more control if you had grown up with it, had more experience navigating it."

"Oh, gods," she said, and threw her head back. "Imagine if teenage boys could change. My kind would be head butting over girls until they concussed, and other species would rip each other's throats out. Literally. No, the knowledge of how to take animal forms is smartly reserved for when we're mature enough to handle it."

"How long until we learn, I wonder."

But what I really longed to know was how long until I discovered whether I slithered or barked.

A

Our third and final class of the day proved to be the most fascinating, but also the most difficult. Metamorphosis was a smaller class of about thirty students since it was hands-on rather than straight lecture like Craft or Cosmology. Groups of four to six students sat on low-backed metal stools around tall rectangular tables. I sat with Timbra, Boone, and Layla, while Bex, Ewan, and the lunar-eyed Raynor shared a table with two other students I didn't know.

"Students, let us get one thing clear right now," barked a spindly bald man in spectacles at the front of the room.

"I will not tolerate nonsense of any kind. None. If any of you think yourselves comedic geniuses or overly intellectual, think again. Finding Your Metamorphosis is more than a college course; it will grant you the defining moment of your young lives.

"Soon we will embark on the most spiritual endeavor of your existence in order to find what physical form your very soul will take. You are undoubtedly familiar with the term 'soul,' the lifeforce of our being. In this class we will discover your soul as animal, or the physical manifestation of your true inner self. Through this course alone you will know the duality of possessing both a static humanoid and an animal form, and I'm the only one that can help you. I suggest you pay attention."

My classmates and I dared not breathe. The only audible sound was the scratching of an ancient wall clock's second hand ground over dull brass numbers by decrepit gears.

"Ah. I see I have your attention," he said. "Let's begin."

Professor Fendrel Martin did, in fact, have our attention. This was the moment we had been waiting for—to learn to reach that part of us linked directly to our evolutionary heritage.

He held a stack of crisp white paper, and as he weaved between tables he distributed an individualized handout to each person in the class. He called out the surnames of the recipients. "Adder, Avenatio, Bartlet, Corleone, Durand…"

Damn alphabetical listings and an "S" name.

"…Redfern…" I had seen Boone, Layla, Ewan, Bex, and then finally Timbra all greedily snatch their stapled papers from the professor's hand and devour its contents. I was dying to get my hands on mine.

"…Stonewall…" My heart stuttered to a stop and I sucked a breath in through my teeth. It took him 900 seconds to get to my desk, and when he finally got close enough I lifted off of my stool and snatched it right out of his hands. He probably gave me a censorious look, but I don't know for sure because once I had the handout in my hands my gaze never left it. My whole identity could be revealed in the next second. All I had to do was turn the page.

The printouts were personalized for each student and listed family histories, genetic anomalies, and other information, as well as the name and contact information for each student's advisor.

Many students shared advisors since genetic classifications intersected. Bex, for example, whose genetic ancestry was that of lions was paired—much to her obvious distaste—with another student whose family evolved from hyenas.

Likewise, Boone and Raynor shared an advisor since they both fell within the scientific suborder Caniformia. I had already learned of Raynor's ancestry of seals. Boone, I was not surprised to learn, was descended of great dogs—ancient Greek Molossians.

"My ancestors chased the beasts of the forests," Boone boasted. "How about you, Bristol?" he asked as he turned on his stool to face Ewan.

"My people *are* the beasts of the forests," Ewan said menacingly. "You wanna have a go now?"

"Ah. No thanks," Boone blew him off with a laugh and a shake of his head, ever the good-natured soul.

"And you, Stella? From what great line are your people descended?"

Of course he had no way to know that this subject was uncomfortable for me. I had not shared with anyone the enigma of my paternity; not even Timbra.

The paper was so starched that I had to lick my finger to flip to the second page. The cover whirred as I threw it over in search of my information.

Except for one line, my handout was blank. The only information listed?

Metamorphosis Advisor: Rowan Gresham

My heart plummeted to the pit of my stomach. I closed my eyes in defeat and anger and let out two or three breaths before I opened them again. I leaned to look at Timbra and Layla's handouts to make sure that mine was, in fact, the anomaly. Of course it was. I knew I wouldn't get any information about myself or my animal form that day. I never answered Boone's question. I was so frustrated I couldn't speak for fear of breaking out in tears.

Professor Martin dismissed the class shortly thereafter with the assignment of making contact with our respective advisors. I really should have seen it coming that Gresham was my advisor. No wonder he had taken such an interest in me. I still had questions, such as how did he know I existed and where to find me. With classes over for the day, I planned to use the remainder of the afternoon to hunt down Gresham and find out. But the best laid schemes, says the old Scots poem, often go awry.

Gresham didn't have an office within the Department of Physical Form, nor did anyone know where he might be. I got the distinct impression that he didn't use an office frequently, if ever. I left the building more than a little irritated. I really wanted some information *about myself* and I was sick of waiting to get it from other people. As I walked back to my room at Sabre Hall I decided to take matters into my own hands.

"Pia, do you have a way to contact Rowan Gresham?"

"Of course, Stella. One moment please."

A real-time image of the man himself appeared on Pia's six-inch screen a moment before he gave a strained, "Gresham." The image came at an odd angle, almost as if his device was lying on the floor…or a bed. All I could see of him was naked, his wide chest and upper torso glistening with a fine sheen of sweat. I knew that he was powerfully built from the way he easily threw me over his shoulder the day of the car wreck. What I never expected was how defined and…and…yummy he would be.

His powerful rounded shoulders bulged and creased along his delts as if straining to hold himself erect. His thick pectorals featured a dusting of chest hair that screamed "*Man.*" What I could see of his upper torso was rigidly corded in muscle. He was built like a fighter. Powerful and lithe.

"Stella. Stella, what's wrong," Gresham was saying.

I realized with a horrified start that I wasn't looking into his eyes, but down the strong lines of his body. I was peeking up and over Pia's screen as if I could get a better, lower view. I glanced quickly up.

"Wrong? No, nothing is wrong. What…what are you doing?" I stammered, aware that I had interrupted some sort of physical exertion.

"I was trying to work out," he huffed, grumpy as ever. "What can I do for you?"

I cleared my throat. And my straying thoughts.

"Why didn't you tell me you were my advisor?" I asked.

"You didn't ask. Do you need something, Stella?"

"I did too ask," I whined, indignant. "I asked why you were helping me and how you found me."

"Okay, I'm helping you because I'm your advisor. It's my job to do so. Does that satisfy you?"

"No. You said you did 'special projects.' Am I a special project?"

He grunted, and the screen moved wildly before coming to a stop at his face. His head tilted forward and his jaw ticked, then he inhaled deeply before continuing.

"Do you know your genetic makeup?"

"Um, no."

"Do you know into what you might turn once you learn how to reach your inner animal form?"

"Nope."

"Do you have any idea how to control yourself while you're in your form?"

"Uh-uh."

"Are you aware of how to shift back into your natural form once turned?"

"Yeah, that's a no."

"Special project," he declared with an imperious nod. "Is that all, Stella? I'm a little busy."

"You answered the phone," I whined, exasperated.

"It's a P.I.A."

"Whatever."

"Goodbye, Stella."

"Wait. I've been assigned to make contact with you. I assume we're supposed to meet and get started on my…transformation?"

"Right," Gresham said with approval and…menace? "Be at my place at 8:00."

"Your home?"

"Yes. Your P.I.A. has my info. I'll see you tonight."

Stella Stonewall
Student Journal Entry #1
Logged via Pia
Monday, May 17

My first day at Radix was, simply put, astounding. Being new not just to Radix, but to Thayer, I may be more overwhelmed than most Root students. The concepts of magic and craft, of an "animal form," and of the need for psychic defense are all completely foreign to me.

I mean, sure, I have read enough fiction to be familiar with magic, but not magic. Like, for real. And it is real; I know that. I felt it the moment I stepped foot in Thayer. It is as if...well, it's like walking in a zero-gravity exhibit—a different reality than I have ever known.

Today in Craft and Ritual Dean Miles cast a spell that made a copy of herself. She called it a 'fetch,' and I suspect she was just showing off, but the fact remains that she made a copy *of herself. Magic. Real magic.*

She may be talented and powerful, but she's also a bully. She belittled me at the front of class, and I cannot fathom why. The only good thing I can say is that I was successful in my recent endeavor to better control my smart mouth.

It's clear that I am going to have to work much harder than everyone else to overcome the learning curve I face. My classmates grew up with magic as a backdrop to their daily lives. Most of their parents and ancestors attended this school and passed on their knowledge. Hell, since animal forms are genetically-informed, most of my friends have a good idea what they'll turn into upon this elusive self discovery.

But because Mom refuses to reveal my father, I have no idea if I'll turn furry or feathery. Shit, what if I'm scaly?

Or horny. Ha. At least I've maintained my sense of humor.

"Stella," interrupted Pia as I typed. "If you need help with humor, please feel free to consult me. I have an extensive repertoire of jokes…that are funny."

"Oh, shut up, Pia. That pun was funny. Anyway, this journal is for my personal use, so as long as I think it's funny that's all that matters. Furthermore, stay out of my journal. These are my private thoughts; I don't need your wisecracks."

Where was I before I was so rudely interrupted?

"Interrupted has two "r's", Stella."

Dammit has two "m's." How about that, Pia? Shut up has two "u's." Hmm? Nothing? I thought so.

Anyway…the one thing that stands out the most in my observations today is the absence of the word "witch" and any religious connotations and applications to the way of life here. Quite a difference from the fundamentalist Christian household I grew up in. It seems that due to the absence of Christianity and even paganism in the historical reference of Thayer, there is only a spiritual ideology that is wholly accepted. It is "animism," I think, and based on the fundamental view that no separation exists between the physical and spiritual worlds and that not just people, but animals, plants, mountains, rivers, storms—everything has a soul or a spirit. It is fascinating and exciting, and I cannot wait to learn more.

*T*here were four free hours between my last class and when I was expected at Gresham's for training. I convinced my new friends to take me into town. They may have grown up around the area, but it was all new to me; I was dying to explore this world.

We left The Root beneath its towering arched gates, walking the mile or so to the main square of the Thayerian capital, Caliph. The ancient city was formed along the Basel River, a source for water, fertile soil, food, and even a port of trade for thousands of years.

Radix was strategically located atop the tallest hill in the area. The winding footpath down into the city provided stunning views of Caliph and the surrounding expanse. The city's architecture reminded me of medieval European cities like Florence and Prague, yet it wasn't cold or crowded. Yellow buildings topped with terra-cotta roofs were broken up occasionally by copper domes gone green with rust. Tree-lined squares and intricate fountains dotted the landscape. I found Caliph to be as breathtaking and magical as everything else I had seen in Thayer.

Across a massive stone structure bridging one city to another was Vischt, Caliph's working-class counterpart. Where

Caliph had the impressive art, architecture, and infrastructure to show for its roots as the cultural and intellectual nucleus of Thayer, Vischt was made up of factories and ports, and the congested housing of blue collar workers.

For a girl that had never left the states, this new world, this city, was wondrously exciting. Radix was unlike any college experience, to be sure, but looking out over a medieval city steeped in history and culture called to me on a cellular level. This place was my home. It was in my bones, my blood. In my very soul.

Once we entered the city's cobbled streets, I was so glad to discover gnomes, dwarfs, and even what I suspected were fairy-like creatures going about their daily business alongside people who looked like me. Though there weren't as many of them as humans, these mystical creatures' existence was still so new and curious to me I was caught staring more than once.

I was *trying* not to be so provincial.

Ewan suggested we eat dinner at a place on Caliph Square that had a large patio. A polite old man seated us with a flourish and took our drink orders.

"I highly recommend the pasta," Ewan said with conviction. "They make it here and serve it perfectly al dente."

"Which pasta?" asked Timbra.

"Any," he said with an easy smile.

After placing our orders, we relaxed with our drinks, chatting and getting to know one another better. Our conversation came with such ease that it seemed no time at all before our food arrived.

I tasted a single bite before sighing in bliss. "Oh. Ewan. You were so right about this pasta," I said between mouthfuls. "I really think it might be the best thing I have ever put in my mouth." His grin reached his eyes before he ducked his head. "I've never had fresh pasta; only the boxed kind," I went on. "The two are so incomparable they should have different names."

The dinner provided an avenue for great conversation, and I learned a lot about my new friends.

"I grew up on a homestead just outside the city," Timbra said. "We grew a lot of our food ourselves. My mother makes the best pasta sauce I've ever tasted. It simmered for hours on our stove, making us so hungry that we never had leftovers, no matter how much she cooked."

"Sounds delicious," I said. "What's her secret?"

"A chopped carrot," Timbra replied, though I never expected to actually discover the secret ingredient.

"We all lived in a big cabin deep in the forest," said Ewan. "I have two sisters and three brothers. Big family. My father always stressed the importance of knowing as much as possible about any subject, every subject. We were taught to work hard and to study hard, and I always enjoyed it. My brothers...well, less so. And while my dad pushed integrity and work ethic, my mom ensured we were polite. She aimed for cultured, she said, but would settle for polite." Ewan's smile took an anguished turn as he talked about his mother.

"I'm sure raising six children was exhausting," I said as I shook my head. "She sounds sweet."

"She was," agreed Ewan. "She died last year. She...she was sick."

"I'm sorry," I said, and I was. What I knew of Ewan's character so far was remarkable. Not being able to meet the woman that raised him felt like a loss.

He quickly steered the conversation away from the subject. "What about you, Adder? You have a big family, too?"

That was the first time that I had considered the connection between dogs, wolves, and...well, litters.

"Oh, yeah," Boone said. "I have several brothers and sisters. We're a rough bunch. Played hard, fought harder, and ran wild in the countryside."

"My childhood was less...conventional," Layla told us. "The Avenatios, we're more magical than most, and my upbringing was steeped in the supernatural."

"What do you mean?" asked Timbra.

"Well, my mother made and sold spells, charms, potions for people. I grew up thinking every kid knew how to grind a turtle shell or find a beehive. It wasn't until I got here that I learned most of you don't know the first thing about magic."

I made a mental note to stick close to Layla in Craft class.

"We rarely had need of magic," professed Bex. "My father is fierce, my mother strong and beautiful. My mom runs things in my family, and appearance and poise was everything to her. She drilled my sisters and me until we ate, drank, and slept deportment. Luckily, she had a lot to work with."

I was still evaluating whether or not anything valuable lay beneath Bex's polished exterior.

"How about you, Stella?" asked Ewan. "What's your family like?"

My heart sank. I didn't have an answer besides my mother. And I really didn't want my new friends feeling sorry for me.

"Oh! Look at the time," I yelped after a quick peek at Pia. "I have an eight o'clock meeting with my advisor. I'm going directly there; I'll see you guys back at The Root. Thank you for this wonderful afternoon."

*P*ia's excellent guidance system, which I termed 'PiaMaps', indicated that Gresham's home was less than a mile from Caliph Square, so I walked in order to see more of the city.

I felt naughty striking out on my own. Exploring beyond Radix's boundaries was both freeing and frightening. Looking up the hillside at the gleaming lights of the Radix campus I was reminded of the magnitude of its history within Thayer, as well as its new role in my life. As gas pathway lamps and well-lit residences shone atop the hill, so too had Radix become a beacon of self-discovery and improvement for me.

But as I left the Square, the inky shadows of nightfall quickly pressed in on me. Before too long I looked over my shoulder at every stray noise. I wished I had asked for a ride; surely someone had a car. But come to think of it, I hadn't seen a single car since entering Thayer. I supposed if one could go anywhere at the speed of thought, there wasn't much use for them. No wonder Gresham went all out when renting a car.

"How much farther, Pia?" I felt like I'd walked three miles.

"Rowan Gresham's house is approximately one hundred yards east. Take your next right."

As I briskly passed the line of neatly maintained brick row houses, I rounded the corner and stopped abruptly, thinking a) *w-o-w*, and b) *this cannot be the right place*. Gresham's house wasn't a house at all, but a manor.

The street ended at massive iron gates anchored by towering stone pillars. A stone wall ran the length of the lane to the gate, so that the property within was obscured from view. Ancient trees rose behind the border and occasionally drooped lazily over it, causing the stones below to grow green with lichen.

I slowed to appreciate the lovely facade and mature landscaping, which included an assortment of herbs and ground cover. I stopped to run lavender, thyme, and mint leaves between my fingers, delighting in the familiar smells. At the manor's entrance, I caught a glimpse of the house beyond and stared, mouth agape, for several moments.

It wasn't opulent or flashy; it was tasteful and classically lovely. Stunning in its symmetry. The marbled beige limestone structure was square, with each of its four corners anchored by two-story square turrets. Paned windows gave the property the feel of a modernized estate, rather than a castle. Several chimneys were visible from the front of the house, stretching from the gray roof toward the stars.

A lot of house for one man. Of course, a manor this size probably required a staff.

I found the iron gates slightly ajar, and sidled in. I knocked nervously on the large front door. In no time, a freshly-showered Gresham greeted me with wet hair and smelling of aftershave.

"Stella. Please, come in."

"Oh, your home is beautiful," I gushed. "If I'm late it's because I was entranced by your garden on the way in."

"Thank you. I've worked for years to get it into shape." Then, almost shyly, "You liked the garden?"

"Oh, yes. What I could see was just lovely, and so well thought out. Do you do some of the work yourself?"

"I do." He nodded and led me through the spacious foyer. "I find the feel of working warm soil in my hands supremely cathartic."

"Yes, I know what you mean. Planting keeps me grounded," I said and his mouth turned up just a bit. "Saw that on a T-shirt." I was nervous. "I know sometimes big houses like this have names. Does this one? Have a name?"

"It does," he said. "Caraway Manor."

"Caraway, like the herb? The seed?"

"Yes. Besides the gardens you may have seen on the way in, I have an heirloom garden out back. I'll show you sometime when it's light out."

"I'd love that. I won't have much opportunity for gardening at Sabre, you know."

"You're welcome here anytime you need to get your hands dirty. Would you like some coffee? A glass of wine before we begin?"

I accepted coffee, and followed him to the kitchen in the back of the house. 'House' was such an inadequate word for the place, but while it was huge and hundreds of years old, it was also warm and lived-in. Plush rugs covered the floors, woven blankets were thrown atop furniture that had obviously been chosen both for utility and style. A set of built-ins covered an entire wall and not just books, but antiquities and interesting trinkets dotted the shelves. It was his home and I loved it; it said a lot about the man who I had found extremely difficult to read.

The kitchen was a generous open space with classic bones and worn hardwood floors, but also top of the line modern appliances, such as a gleaming copper oven. It was a chef's dream kitchen, and I wondered if he cooked. My impression so far was that he was something of a Renaissance man. My guess was that he did.

"Sugar? Cream?" Gresham asked as he poured us two steaming cups of coffee from a French press.

We sat at a comfortable banquette surrounded by the windows facing the back gardens. An open window allowed a soft breeze to deliver cool evening air redolent of soil and lavender. I closed my eyes to savor the extravagant pleasures of my surroundings and the taste of gourmet coffee still hot on my tongue. When I opened my eyes, unaware of how long they'd been closed, Gresham was staring at me, head cocked to the side, with a look of...wonder on his face. In the absence of judgment or mirth on his part, I felt no embarrassment and simply smiled up at him. After a beat he shook himself and began my lesson.

"Stella, the important thing to remember in the search for your animal form is that only you can find it. All the special tutoring in Thayer cannot access that door within you unless you open it yourself mind and body."

"I am open to it," I started defensively, but caught myself. Took a breath. "I just don't know the first place to begin."

"I know. That's why we're here. And I know the concept will be especially difficult for you. You face a significant learning curve, but if you're open-minded and committed, and give yourself over to the possibility of this magic, then you'll find it as surely as anyone."

His confidence was contagious and fortifying. Deep down I knew I could do it; I just hadn't the first clue *how*.

"All right, now stand up," he instructed as he left his own seat to join me. The soft cotton of his black T-shirt allowed the faintest of outlines of his strong chest and shoulders. His charcoal trousers were looser than usual and hung low on his hips. His relaxed-at-home look? My thoughts vaulted back to the image of his glistening chest and abs that I glimpsed on Pia's screen. I forced my gaze away, shaking my head to clear the raw sexiness of the man who was now effectively my teacher.

Unsure of the dress code for learning one's inner beast at a hot older guy's place after eight, I had pulled my hair up in a loose chignon and chosen a classic ensemble. I paired a black polka-dot dress with an olive green handbag and shoes. A thin black belt cinched the narrow waist. This was my go-to first date outfit, but he didn't have to know that.

Gresham stood close—too close—behind me and lay his fingertips lightly atop my shoulders.

"Close your eyes, Stella."

I did, though with hesitation. I felt vulnerable. And a bit silly.

He leaned forward to speak soothingly at my ear. "Now, breathe in deeply, Stella, and try to see in your mind's eye your source of power. Some people picture this chakra as their actual heart; some as a radiating source of light. Whatever you imagine that cache of power to be, concentrate on the physical appearance of it."

I had taken several yoga classes over the course of my college years. This was, of course, unbeknown to my mother, who believed her preacher when he taught that meditation left a soul open to the influence of demons. I had always found the breathing exercises extremely relaxing, and practical in a stressful environment like college sometimes was. The devil had not made his way into my subconscious, to my knowledge.

I utilized this yogi experience and breathed in solidly through my nose. I blew out through slightly pursed lips. As I breathed, I recalled my first glimpse of my chakra in Craft class.

In through the nose; out through the mouth.

Thinking about Craft made me think of Dean Livia Miles.

In through the nose; out through the mouth.

Thinking of Dean Miles made me wonder how many times she had sat at this very table for breakfast after an overnight at Gresham's.

In through the nose; out through the mouth.

Thoughts of Dean Miles and Gresham being intimate gave me a sick feeling in the pit of my stomach, which was so not the place I was supposed to be concentrating.

With a sharp exhale, I opened my eyes and turned to face Gresham.

"Sorry. My mind keeps wandering," I said, dejected.

"It's all right," he assured me with a nod of his head. "You'll get this. It isn't supposed to be easy. There's a reason students are taught technique in class, as well as by a hands-on advisor. Do you want to try again, or would you prefer to break for a bit?"

I turned back around and closed my eyes in silent indication. "Good girl. Now, start your breathing again. That was good."

As I breathed in and out, actively clearing my mind of thought, of outside sources of angst or worry, Gresham's hands once again landed lightly on my shoulders. I could've sworn he'd moved even closer behind me. The sound of his soft breathing, the feel of his breath as he exhaled above my neck soon took over my thoughts and dashed my efforts to clear my mind. I began concentrating on the feel of the minuscule vibrations of the hairs at the back of my neck. A heated weight formed deep in my belly; my body telling me there was a vacant space yearning to be filled. I knew that feeling, though it had been some time since I'd felt it; and certainly not just by the innocent contact of breath on my nape. Eyes closed, I delighted in the feeling, and let my mind wander. I could almost feel him leaning into me, his lips not just blowing air onto my neck, but leisurely kissing me there. I wanted to feel the heat of his body, those strong pectorals against my back. Instinctively I arched my back, reaching for that contact but stopped short just in time.

I was embarrassed that I'd almost backed up to him like a cat in heat. My cheeks were hot with shame, as well as the beginning stirrings of irritation. Was Gresham's contact innocent? I tried to imagine Timbra or even Boone's advisors standing this closely to them, touching their shoulders ever-so-softly. I doubted they were facing the same scenario that I was. Further, I doubted they were being tutored after hours at the home of their advisor. What had I been thinking? What was *Gresham* thinking? Did he invite me here to teach me to find my inner self, or to get near me? The more I thought about it, the stupider I felt. And when I remembered the fact that he was seeing someone, I did get pissed.

Jerking out of Gresham's reach I turned on him, my gaze throwing darts. To his credit, he was startled and, I did note, flaccid. Still, I thought it best to re-evaluate what I had gotten myself into.

"I think that's enough for tonight, Gresham," I said as I grabbed the wooden handle of my handbag.

"All right, Stella. We'll go at the pace that you feel most comfortable. A good effort tonight; a good beginning," he said.

Still wary, I thanked him for the coffee and complimented his lovely home. I passed briskly by the statued fountain and toward the black iron gate.

I decided what I really needed was a beer, and imagined my next footfall landing outside Sabre Bar.

I did it, no problem. That little feat went a long way to lighten my mood, as did spotting my friends surrounding a high pub table near the dartboard. I ordered a beer from Knox, avoiding his attempt to chat me up.

A few beers and a few rounds of darts put the night's events in perspective. I realized with no small sense of shame that Gresham had not actually come on to me; I had let my raging hormones cloud my judgment. Good lord, I had to get a grip on my libido before I embarrassed myself further.

So the man invited me to his lovely estate and served me coffee. At night. Big deal. So he stood fairly close behind me and touched my shoulders. So what. He had told me on more than one occasion that Root students were all consenting adults; not college kids. The fact was that I let my own overwhelming attraction to him freak me out.

Before crashing into my new favorite place—my comfy bed—I resolved not to get in the way again of my much-needed education on all things mystical.

Stella Stonewall
Student Journal Entry #2
Logged via Pia
Monday, May 31

I am frustrated to report I have had no real progress toward finding my animal form. After discovering that the key lay in my chakra, I have practiced flexing it, so to speak, and can say with confidence that I understand it, and consequently, myself, a little better. That's all I got, really, at this point.

Despite her poor treatment of me, Dean Miles is unquestionably intelligent and talented. I have taken her advice to heart, and am seeking any and all knowledge that I can acquire. I have thrown myself into books and classes, interviewing my professors at length for more information. At first they were delighted in my interest, but now I fear they find me irritating. Doesn't matter. I read and I research and I practice.

I have never feared hard work. I WILL close the gap on the advantage that my classmates have on me.

Oh, and for what it's worth, I totally made it longer than a week. Those suckers making bets I wouldn't last lost. Big time.

hen it came to exercise, I typically preferred to run out of doors or do yoga at home. But Timbra had convinced me to go with her to an indoor cycling class, insisting that exercise infused with magic was not to be missed.

The instructor, a knockout brunette with the widest gap between her thighs I had ever seen in real life, was a gifted illusionist. As the up-tempo beat-laden music thumped through the room, she first wove a scene for warm-up. Speaking into a wireless headset to be heard over the music, she relayed our intent for a four-minute warm-up along the Basel River.

As she described the gray water flowing along the serene banks, I was transported from the sweaty gym onto a river trail. She continued to speak, but her words faded away and in their place was the feel of cool wind on my brow as I began to perspire. A hawk "cawed" overhead and splashed into the river, its dive for a long slender fish successful. I continued to pedal through the warm-up at an even pace, my heart rate steadily increasing.

As I rounded a copse of trees, the music in the background changed to one with an urgent beat. A steep hill lay directly in my path. In order to make it up the daunting obstacle, I left the bike's saddle and stood, pedaling in time with that driving beat. I pushed myself harder and harder, pedaling as if my life depended on it. My leg muscles screamed for respite, but still I pedaled. Near-breathless, I reached the top of the hill, and when I looked to the valley below the scenery changed.

The ocean's endless expanse lay to my right. At a leisurely pace I followed a sidewalk and listened to the soothing ebb and swell of the sea as gentle waves crashed onto the deserted beach. The sun beat down, and it was wonderful, cleansing. I sipped water from a bottle on my bike's frame.

The sandy beach became rocky terrain. The only trail in sight was overgrown and rocky, and my road bike was no match for it. I moved to re-attach my water bottle and when I looked down I sat atop a mountain bike. As I stood again to navigate the rough forest terrain, my surroundings became oppressive. Enormous trees formed a canopy so dense that sunlight fought to stream through. Sparse rays shot toward the forest floor, illuminating dust particles that pirouetted through their brilliance. I could hear the brief, hurried scampering of small animals as my approach frightened them away. The fresh woody redolence of the forest, the earthen scent of fallen leaves as they crunched beneath my chunky tires gave me great pleasure, even as I struggled to keep up the fast pace. The forest trail became less and less passable as I progressed, the underbrush at some places tearing angry red scratches across my calves. I had pedaled so long and at such a consistent incline that my energy level neared spent. My breaths left in ragged huffs and I began to feel lightheaded.

Luckily, the terrain changed once more, placing me at…my old neighborhood. I wondered how the talented instructor had ever formed this scene. Was she accessing my memories? It made me a little uncomfortable to consider, but my unease was soon forgotten as my old friends joined me on the street. I pedaled leisurely atop a vintage orange cruiser. It was my bike from my childhood with a basket in front and a broken kickstand—every detail was right. I laughed aloud with other giggling girls as an older boy showed out, popping a wheelie and then crashing as he overestimated his ascent. My basket held a Coke bottle and I slugged it, savoring the syrupy taste of real sugar.

Too soon this scene was replaced with another challenging course. I forced out the last remaining energy I possessed to complete it, so relieved to hear the words "cool down" and a reggae song replace the pulsing electronic beat. Rolling my neck and drinking my water, the gym class came into view once more.

I found Timbra immediately and mouthed "Oh. My. God." She smirked; I could practically read her mind—*Told ya so.*

After class I approached Pippa, the instructor.

"That was so amazing. I've never experienced anything like that. Thank you so much."

"Oh, I'm glad you enjoyed it," she gushed. Her face was flushed, her tight exercise top as soaked with perspiration as the rest of ours.

"This was my first time. How did you create my childhood street and friends? How is that possible?"

"Trade secret," she replied, tapping a finger to her temple.

Stella Stonewall
Student Journal Entry #3
Logged via Pia
Monday, June 7

The past three weeks have flown by! I am shocked by the mountains of new information that I have learned with each class. My Tuesday/Thursday classes (Tools of the Trade, Elements, and Herbalism) have opened my eyes to so much more that I need to learn. And my Wednesday night Breaking Bad lab is going to be a lifesaver. I am learning how to protect myself from physical or mental attacks.

The overarching theme for me right now is self-awareness. I am horrified at how little I know about myself and my abilities. Every time I think about the shallow little existence I have lived up to this point... Shit, I just cringe.

I mean, sure, I'm a typical college kid. I've been ashamed to discover, though, that I've never even tried to scratch the surface of who I really am.

"After a time skin sags; appearance fades," a favorite professor told me on my twenty-first birthday. "Look deeper," she said.

At the time, I thought that sounded exactly like something a fifty-year-old spinster would say—what else did she have? But with each new day at Radix, I'm learning that the true strengths of a person cannot be found externally. True beauty can be found in a cherished friendship, in small acts of kindness, in self-exploration and education, and in the confidence that results from all these.

Beauty, however, is not what I am charged with discovering now. No, my directive at Radix, and as a new-found Thayerian, is to find power within myself. Power to shield against those that would harm me, power to find the physical form of my soul, power to manipulate the world around me—to do magic.

I t was my sixth meeting with Gresham. We met twice
a week—on Monday nights, while the Metamorphosis
class was still fresh, and again on Thursday afternoons. I'd
proved successful in reining myself in and not climbing his tall
ass like a tree. The thought crossed my mind once. Okay,
twice. Hell, at every meeting—the important part was that I
refrained.

He remained professional, and while he was often cranky,
he did have rare moments of pleasant and sometimes even
approached cheerful. I never knew which Gresham I would
encounter, but since I couldn't change who I was anyway, I
usually chatted away merrily as he shared his insight on how to
release my form.

"Dammit, Stella!" Gresham roared behind me. I jerked
clumsily away, scrabbling for purchase of a nearby bench. We'd
been practicing outside, the weather fair and his back yard
lovely. I searched his face, thinking I had elbowed him in the
nose or stepped on his toe—hurt him somehow. But, no. He
was *frustrated* with me. For the first time, to my knowledge.
He'd been patient, and I thought we'd been making real
progress.

"What the hell, Gresham?" My voice came out in a higher pitch than I'd intended.

"Focus, Stella." he said, rounding on me with clenched fists. "Do you think this is a game? You act as if this is all cotton candy and rainbows and that you have all the time in the world to prepare for what's coming. If you aren't committed to this, stop wasting my time. I certainly have more important things to do than play tutor to a silly little girl. If you'd pull your head out of that tight little ass for one moment you'd realize this is important. The sooner you discover your form, the sooner you can learn to control it. And when you can control it, you can use it to protect yourself."

O-kaaaaay. I guessed we were bypassing cranky and going straight on through to deranged and conspiratorial.

But to insinuate I wasn't serious, that I was being lazy, was going too far. I was infuriated. And, 'silly little girl'? Well, that was just mean.

"First of all," I said, stepping into his personal space with fists clenched at my waist so tightly my nails dug into my palms. "I have no idea what you're talking about. What do I need to protect myself from? And what's the hurry? You said we could go at my own pace. Why this shit fit now? And furthermore, I am *committed!* While my friends are out having fun, you know where I am? In my room, spending all my time reading, studying everything I can get my hands on to catch up to what they learned at home. I may've had a disadvantage when I came here, but I'm so far ahead in most of my classes that I could teach them."

He rolled fierce honeyed eyes at me, an action which made them far less attractive, though the pull of his angry mouth and the sharp lines of his gaze did scream 'dangerously sexy'. Or just 'dangerous.' Or just 'sexy.' Damn, I was hopeless.

"Oh, please," he scoffed, leaning so that he towered over me. I had to look up to see his face. "You haven't even scratched the surface of the knowledge you need. And after three weeks with you, I'm not convinced you even *have* another form. All the books in the world can't teach you to control raw power, Stella. You can't possibly know what it means to coax a throbbing chakra; to fan its banked fire until, white hot, energy bursts forth and burns forcibly through your veins. You can't imagine the rush you'll feel when the only physical form you've ever known explodes into a thousand pieces and leaves a monster in its wake. And the liberating part about changing is that you don't even care. You're free; you're...*yourself*—finally."

Gresham stopped then, a stray thought obviously taking hold as he eyed me in appraisal.

"What?" I pouted.

"Nothing."

"Tell me, Gresham. Why hold back now?"

"Oh, I assure you that I have held back," he said, disdain dripping from his voice.

"Look, despite what you think, I *am* trying." I slumped back down on the bench, my hands falling loosely to my lap. "It's just that this entire thing is so foreign to me that I can't grab hold. I mean, I understand the concept of it, sure, but putting it into practice is my hangup." I slapped the bench with both hands in frustration, reveling in the sting. "And that's why you were assigned to me, right? To help me with the physical part of my metamorphosis? I haven't the faintest idea how to 'coax a throbbing chakra,' for gods' sake."

He'd gone still as stone, though his gaze still followed me. "I just thought of one way," he said. "But it's unconventional and I'm not sure you're...up for it."

"Gresham, you just chewed my ass and questioned my commitment. If you know of a way to help me, do it. I'm a big girl." I took a deep breath and squared my shoulders. "I can handle it."

"All right," he agreed, though still hesitant. "But if you find the subject matter offensive, remember you asked for it. For now, just go with it."

"I can do that," I said. "Shoot."

A

"Have you ever orgasmed, Stella?"

Whaaah? I nearly fell off the bench. I was sure glad he had suggested I sit, or I would have fallen over completely.

"Ah, that's a pretty personal question." No way was I talking to him about that.

"The sensations are related," he said, exasperated. "I need to know if you have had an orgasm so that I can explain to you the similarities. If you've never had one, then the explanation is pointless."

I started to say 'who hasn't?,' but I already knew the answer to that. I personally knew a *few* girls. As impossible as it was for me to believe it, late-night, tequila-drunk, college girl talk had revealed some of my own friends had never orgasmed-- through intercourse or otherwise. They blamed religious or parental guilt, and certainly their partners' skill levels. "*What about, you know, 'alone time'?*" I'd asked. These same girls couldn't seem to shake the shame or the shyness to *help themselves.* And certainly I couldn't see them in a novelty shop acquiring mechanical assistance.

But to the conversation at hand, I didn't care to reveal too much and simply replied, "Yes. I have."

"Excellent." He nodded in approval. All business.

But then he lowered his head down to mine, scooting near me on the bench so that mere inches separated our faces; our noses so close that I could feel the warmth of his skin. He smelled so good. I let my eyes drift closed to savor the faintest hint of cologne mingled with the natural scent of his skin.

"Do you know that moment," he half spoke, half whispered, gaze intent on my own, "when you feel that familiar quickening low in your body? That first inkling of knowledge that if things keep going this well, if you can just reach a little farther, that you're sure to peak?" His eyes searched mine for the assurance that I did know what he meant.

I had to clear my throat twice to get out a shaky "I know it."

"Yes," he said, his voice deepening and his eyes crinkling at the corners with amusement and...interest? "It appears you do."

The baldness of his questions, the proximity of his big body to mine, and his breath on my face that smelled minty yet sweet, like cloves, already had my engine revved. My breathing had become heavy; my chest rose and fell roughly with each breath.

His lips parted at my response. "You know what I'm talking about don't you, Stella? Can you imagine yourself right now in that moment, just on the precipice of of your body exploding into a million pieces?"

"Yes," I breathed, eyes closed. My god, it was way better than phone sex.

"Good girl," he said, and hearing the words sent a thrill sliding down my spine.

"Now imagine not your...not your lower body, but your chakra; that place just outside your heart. Your chakra: your body's true center. Imagine your chakra pulsing and throbbing, desirous of attention."

Truthfully, I didn't *want* to move from my throbbing lady parts to my chakra, but I understood the importance of the exercise. Reluctantly, I reached out with my mind, an imaginary palm moving slowly upward to rest above my breastplate. There. Faint, but there. It wasn't a throbbing, but a thrumming, like when one gets too close to an electrical plant and can feel the vibrations of electrical current.

"I feel it." I whispered emphatically, my breaths becoming shallow, quick.

"Good," he said. "Good. Now, relay your memories from a sexual context to this psychic one. Concentrate on the quickening of your chakra, reach just a little further. Imagine yourself opening up, your inner being thickening and softening, becoming pliable and ready for this new experience."

And, god, I could. My insides grew weighted and expanded, anticipating the next directive. I nodded my head, unable to speak, unwilling to break the spell.

"Yes, Stella. Perfect. Now, zero in on that one concentration of psychic power that's your chakra—the clitoris of the soul, so to speak."

"Imagine it catching fire and burning white hot. Yes, now, when I say, picture the entire chakra erupting into a massive explosion that forces its way through your veins and pours into your every organ. Are you ready?"

I could only vaguely nod, mouth agape in concentration.

"Now, Stella." At his words not my body, but my *soul*, bucked, eviscerating barriers that until then had been untouched. I imagined a tiny hole forming in the thick, rubbery constraint, and then, like a beacon, my white-hot fire shined through. I singed a hole big enough for my inner being to escape, cauterizing my way through to allow access of every single atom of my physical form. Saliva pooled in the back of my throat as if I might be sick, but it wasn't my stomach's contents that wanted out of my body; it was my soul's physical form.

Instead of nausea there was excruciating pain. A massive clawed thing was fighting within me to escape. Hell, it felt like several massive clawed things were fighting against each other, my body painfully wrenched this way and that from the force of their attacks. My head fell back as I cried out. My arms crossed protectively over my stomach, and I fell to my knees panting through the pain.

Gresham seemed to realize then that something had gone horribly wrong and dropped down beside me.

"That's enough for now, Stella," he said in a calming tone, though when I rose up to howl again I saw the briefest flare of panic in his eyes.

"Let's put her back to rest for now," he said. "Follow my instructions; can you do that?"

I could only nod, still panting through the pain like a laboring mother.

"Good girl. Now, imagine your chakra gradually and gracefully mending itself. Instead of flowering, picture it folding in like a hibiscus bloom at dusk."

118

Still on his knees beside me, he reached over to gently smooth my hair. He continued to say soothing things, praising my good work and rubbing my back in slow, supportive circles. I worked hard to calm myself, to rein in my frantic pulse.

Finally, as if the gaping tear had healed, I felt normal again and breathed a deep, cleansing breath. I looked up at Gresham, giving him a quick nod to indicate that I was better, and rose upright. I put my hands on my thighs and sat on my haunches a while, recovering.

"Was that normal?" I asked once I was able to speak. I was weak, and the words came out in a croaked whisper.

"When it comes to finding one's physical form, there is no normal. Each person, each form is different."

"You know what I'm asking, Gresham. I saw fear in your eyes."

"Well, most times releasing an animal form for the first time is difficult, and sometimes a bit painful. You were in substantial pain, though, which is unusual."

"It felt...how can I explain this? It felt like things were clawing not at me, but at *each other* to get out. Does that make sense?"

Gresham nodded noncommittally. He was hiding something.

"What? What is it?"

"Nothing, Stella. You did well today. You did so well, in fact, that I am sure you're exhausted. Let's get you home." He ran his arm across my back and held on to my shoulder, transporting me to the comfort of my room with a single thought.

Stella Stonewall
Student Journal Entry #4
Logged via Pia
Thursday, June 10

What the hell just happened?

With Gresham's help I FINALLY discovered how to manipulate my chakra and access my animal form. His methods were…unconventional, to say the least, but they were effective. I felt my form within me. It wanted O.U.T. And I wanted to let it fly. But suddenly I sensed that something held it back. I don't know what.

I do know that it hurt like hell, and I suspect that's not a typical occurrence. Gresham's reaction frightened me. Though he wouldn't say it, I think something went wrong. Bad wrong.

Gah! This is all so frustrating. I feel that if I could just picture what it is that I am trying to release, then I would be exponentially more successful.

My next plan of attack is…more practicing. More studying. More research. Though, if I am honest I'll admit that at this moment I am not looking forward to trying to reach my form again. Pain is a very powerful deterrent.

"*B*ut, Stella, I *can't* date him, don't you see?" In fact I did not see. Over the course of several weeks, I had deduced that big, playful, powerful Boone Adder had it bad for my suitemate, and I knew she was into him, too. My efforts to facilitate the match had been rebuffed at every turn, and I was getting sick of seeing them moon longingly at each other when they thought no one was looking. I thought they should just make out like teenagers and get it over with.

Timbra then explained to me that dating and, relatedly, procreating in Thayer was different than in the world I knew.

In Thayer, genetics weren't just histories, they were legacies. As human species had descended from so many sources, not just apes, evolution was taken very seriously. Proud forbearers had demanded from the dawn of time that sons and daughters find mates only within their species, and for good reason. Viable offspring couldn't be produced between two people so genetically disparate as, say, those of cervid and canine descent.

I had learned in a biology course that mules, the offspring of male donkeys and female horses, were born sterile because of the two species' differing number and structure of chromosomes. This sounded a little like that.

"Wait a minute," I said, throwing my hands up in distressed disbelief. I sat cross-legged on Timbra's vintage braided rug. "Are you telling me that you and…well, everybody here, are limited to relationships only within your species? You can only have sex with guys who are deer?"

"Ohhhh, no, no, no," she assured me.

"Whew."

"Yeah, people hook up interspecies all the time. I mean, this is college, and some people have never spent any time with someone outside their species. We're all adults here. You combine curiosity with booze and private rooms, and the result is some strange bed partners. Bex, for example, has raised her tail for the entire soccer team. That wouldn't be so bad if she didn't insist on scent marking every one of her conquests. They finally caught on when no other girls would come near them. After that, a lot of guys avoid her like the clap, but Bex is Bex and will never be alone for long."

I definitely agreed with her there. Bex was one of those girls that exuded sexy/trashy, which some…no, *a lot* of men found irresistible.

"Okay then. If hooking up is accepted, why can't you and Boone get together? It's not like anyone is looking for a mate. Are you? And if, as you say, you can't make a baby, then what's the harm?"

"Well, I just don't believe that I should date anyone with whom there's no future," she said. "What's the point, ya know? Besides, I tend to fall pretty hard, and I like Boone so much that I know I would eventually get hurt."

Yes, I could see the same quality that made Timbra such a good friend could also put her at risk of heartache. She was kind and gentle and generous; her heart was open and her demeanor unassuming. I hoped she did find someone wonderful as a mate, but she also deserved happiness right now. I knew she pined for Boone, but I'd said my piece. It was her business, and I respected her opinion.

"All right, I get it," I said and blew out a breath. "But at least tell me who else is hooking up; I haven't been around much to see it. Somebody besides Bex should be getting laid around here, and it sure isn't you or I."

Timbra's eyes lit at that. Like me she delighted in juicy news.

"Well, Layla is getting biz-zee on the regular with that busty waitress from Sabre Bar. The blonde? And, I can't prove anything, but I suspect Raynor is getting more ass than a coffee house toilet seat. According to Boone, women practically throw their va-jay-jays at him. But you know what they say abou…"

"Stop." I said. "Did you just say 'va-jay-jay?'"

"Um. Yeah." Her long black eyelashes blinked in confusion.

"No. Just. No." My eyes squinted in disgust.

"Well, what do you call it? I can hardly say vagina; I'd sound like my grandmother."

"Well I don't know. Lady bits? The grandest canyon? Notorious V.A.G.?"

I cracked myself up on that one and rolled onto my side laughing at the scandalized look on Timbra's face. I was on a roll, though, and continued to spout ridiculous names as they came to me until it was obvious by Timbra's huffed breaths that I had passed funny and gone right on to obnoxious. Something I'm working on.

"All right, I'm sorry," I said. "I call it 'my girl,' but have been known to even refer to it as 'pussy' in the heat of the moment." 'Pussy' was used sparingly and always whispered, as befitting its naughty station.

"What about Ewan?" I asked to change the subject. God knew I wanted him. Surely he was getting some action.

Timbra's head snapped up at that, her slender ears twitching. I should have known she'd be uber perceptive. "Why do you care who Ewan's doing?"

"I don't," I shrugged. "We've just covered everyone else, and I'm curious."

She didn't buy that for a second. She eyed me with doubt and said. "I've seen him spending time with Pippa Sterling."

"Pippa? The spin instructor?"

"That's the one," she agreed, eyes wide in mock outrage.

"Good for them," I said, though the last thing I felt was generous upon contemplation of her high, tight bottom and steely abs.

Timbra shrugged in apology, but perked up. "It's sangria and soul food night downstairs."

God, I loved her.

A

Sabre Bar was hoppin'. It was Friday, so the music was loud and so were the patrons, who were letting off steam after a tough week of classes. Timbra and I joined right in, ordering a round of shots for ourselves and our little group, which we spotted in a corner. After a quick toast 'to our metamorphoses,' we settled in to comfortable conversation and frequent bursts of laughter. Since the topic was broached, I took the opportunity to quiz Layla, Boone, Ewan, and Bex about their progress with their animal forms.

I already knew Timbra was well on her way to mastering hers, which was—no surprise—a large deer species. As a doe, her form had not given much fight. Once she learned to release it, it simply leapt from within her. She described the experience in terms of rebirth—that she was new and whole for the first time, as if she had been searching for something her entire life, and when she finally found it, she pulled it around herself like a favorite sweater.

To say I was envious was a serious understatement. Not only did I not know my genetic background or my father, I had no idea what my form would be. And that last exercise with Gresham had only served to scare the hell out of me. I had since been unable to achieve the same level of connection, fear overriding my desire to face my metamorphosis. Gresham had been patient, but I could tell was again nearing frustration with me.

"Layla, how goes your search for your form?" I asked.

Layla handled everything with an air of confidence and indifference. "Well, when your form is a crow, it's not that hard to handle, Stonewall."

I hadn't known her form was a crow. That certainly explained the tattoo.

"And you, Boone?" I knew he was descended of massive ancient hunting dogs, but I hadn't heard if he had learned to manipulate it.

"I succeeded just today. That's part of what we're celebrating tonight."

"Oh, congratulations!" I said at the same time Layla piped in with a smirk.

"Took you long enough, dog."

"Listen," Boone said. "When you're as big as me, you have to take your time. You can't just ram roughshod. No, a big man like me has to take things nice and slow. The result, though, is always worth the wait."

We all knew it was innuendo, and he delivered it so well that when he finished, we just smiled and shook our heads. I sneaked a look at Timbra, curious if she thought him as cheeky as the rest of us.

The poor girl was so gone. It was obvious, though probably only to me, that she was thinking hard about being on the receiving end of his largess. I gave her a sharp elbow to the gut and a pointed look. She had the good sense to look abashed, and I could only shake my head, knowing that she refused to act on her interest.

"Bex and Ewan found their forms weeks ago," Layla relayed, unfazed. "I hear Ewan's was a sight to behold." I knew they had; but I hadn't heard details. Some people found the process deeply personal while others, like Boone and Layla, let it all hang out.

"Oh?" My interest was piqued about Ewan's form and I turned in my seat to look expectantly in his direction. I knew little about his family…little about him at all, really. He was so reserved that he seemed eternally introspective. And while his whole 'brooding' thing was intriguing, I was beginning to suspect that it was a device to keep from revealing much about himself.

Ewan smiled shyly at me, his dark gaze meeting mine before turning down. I reached to smooth along his jaw, his perpetual five-o-clock shadow rasping beneath my fingers. With my thumb just at the edge of his mouth, I drew his face up to meet my gaze again. His eyes were wide, shocked at the intimacy of my touch. I was also shocked and looked, stunned, at my hand, wondering how it had arrived there. *Damned sangria.* "Ah. I'm sorry... I don't know what..." I sputtered and jerked my hand back to my lap just as Bex cut in.

"My lioness was powerful and glorious," she announced, throwing her long caramel hair behind a shoulder. "The Corleones are notoriously kindred with our forms. Once I opened myself up to her, she leapt out with ferocity."

I gave a weak, "That's great," as some of the others 'mmm'ed' noncommittally.

"Still no progress, Stella?" Boone asked. I had not discussed my difficulty with anyone, and was a little embarrassed to learn that they all knew anyway.

"I've had progress," I protested. "I came very close recently, but had some...problems and had to stop before my form was released. I haven't gotten that far again."

"It helped me to think of my form symbiotically," Ewan said softly. "Not as a force trying to escape my body, but as a part of me that I willingly released. Sometimes the more you fight it, the more difficult the process is."

"Yeah, I get that. I'm really trying," I said. "It's just tough for me. You all know your ancestry and have at least a general idea what form to envision. Not knowing what to concentrate on releasing is...well, it's scary, as well as difficult."

"You'll get there, girl." This from Layla, who spoke in my direction, but whose gaze followed our waitress as she approached.

"Another round?" Mari, our small but curvy server, encouraged. As she cleared empties she moved around our table, shooting occasional heated glances at Layla. They weren't revealing their relationship, but were doing little to conceal it, either.

My ears rang and I had a familiar sense of foreboding as images flashed in the periphery of my vision. A scratchy, flickering projection revealed Mari tripping on an upturned rug corner and sending the tray of empty glasses flying across our table. I'd had one or two of these premonitory visions before, and they always happened mere seconds before the event occurred.

Coursework in divining was reserved for sophos or higher, but I'd suspected that the precognitive urges I'd had leading up to my entry to Thayer might have been the beginning manifestations of my innate abilities. I'd studied the topic at length. It wasn't just theorized, but had been proven in rare instances that, if the vision was received well enough in advance, the outcomes of any given event could be changed.

On a whim, I decided to test the theory. When Mari approached Timbra's side, I rose from my chair. Just as I neared her, Mari tripped on the rug. I reached out to stabilize her, she gained control of the tray, and then nodded to me in thanks.

"Whew, that was close! Thanks, Stella."

"No problem. Right place at the right time," I said numbly as I tried to accept what had just happened.

"You're all going to Solstice Fest, right?" Mari asked, abandoning her duties to chat for the moment.

"Wouldn't miss it," Boone said. "I'm going to check out some of the bands, and eat my weight in festival food."

"When is it?" I tried to rejoin the conversation. I would contemplate my newfound talent later. Much later.

I'd heard some talk of the celebration surrounding the summer solstice, but surely it wasn't anytime soon. Could it be mid-June already?

"This Saturday," Timbra chimed in. "You're going. Layla's band plays at nine."

"You're in a band?" I squeaked. Totally fit, though.

"Mm-hmm," Layla nodded. "Shiny Things. Me and some people I know from back home."

"They're really good," Mari said. Layla smiled at her sweetly and gave a slow blink in thanks.

"What else goes on besides music and food?" This was all new to me, and very exciting. Getting off campus for a while sounded perfect.

*B*y Friday, the entire campus was abuzz in anticipation of the Solstice Festival. More than just the longest day of the year, which was practically all the information that my Bible Belt upbringing had afforded me, Summer Solstice, or Midsummer, was a celebration of the end of planting and the beginning of harvest. It was a time to celebrate fertility, and when the mischievous and malicious were thought to come out to play.

Though the city of Caliph had many squares where people gathered and traded, like those I'd read about in Europe, Caliph Square was the largest. The open-air market was overflowing with tents and food carts…and people. I hadn't expected that many people.

Merchants hawked beer, mead, birch wreaths, and fertility devices of all sorts. Timbra had insisted that we arrive early to check out the booths, and see some hokey rituals and performances. I soon discovered what she really wanted was to score as much festival food as possible. By noon, she had already taken down a funnel cake, some fried cheese curd, a tater twister, and jerk tofu. Vegetarian fair food was a real oxymoron to a turkey leg-lover like me.

We listened to tribal drumming, perused folk art, ate more food, and saw plenty of skin—fertility apparently synonymous with sexuality.

A

In the early afternoon the crowd thickened. People flowed in the direction of the stage, which had been erected on the banks of the river.

"What's going on over there?" I asked Timbra.

"Oh. Yes, you'll want to see that," she nodded soberly.

"What? What is it?"

"A play. A reenactment, really. Each year, the Steward Massacre is reenacted to honor our fallen and to remind us of what's at stake...and what's still out there."

We made our way to the grassy seating area just in time. As the production began, Gnomes and winged Fae—they didn't want to be called fairies, but Fae, Timbra had admonished—worked farmland together in worn tunics and breeches. Heartier built Dwarfs loaded crops onto the backs of wagons drawn by miniature beasts of burden that resembled water buffalo. The creatures worked dutifully, if happily, joining together in songs that illustrated the simple pleasures of working the soil.

When the workday concluded the creatures returned to their families, life peaceful and contented at hearth and home. A new day brought about more good work.

Then, one Fae's ear twitched. She had heard something and looked to a male across the field who confirmed her concern. With no further warning, a monstrous dragon dove overhead, releasing a deafening roar and scorching the crops in the field. The Gnomes, Fae, and Dwarfs let out cries of terror and ran for their lives, diving under wagons and running into the forest. More dragons ravaged the sky, seeking out the hiding creatures after they had destroyed the crops and farmland. One by one the dragons ferreted out the small beings—their children, too—and set them ablaze, their excruciated shrieks filling the air before stopping altogether.

The crowd that had gathered for the reenactment sat stunned, silent, *moved*. I dragged in a ragged breath, on the verge of tears at the gruesome sight that I knew had actually occurred, yet on a much larger scale. Timbra discreetly wiped her eyes and gazed into her lap in silent despair.

The scene on stage changed. A dragon lay in a mountain lair, lethargic and desolate. The costume had been exceptionally made, the ruby eyes striking and intelligent. A young-looking man approached the beast and praised it for its work. The dragon closed its eyes in shame and turned away. The man reached to pet its mighty head.

"There, there, my beast. No sense regretting what cannot be changed. You serve me now."

For the first time, I noticed a thick metal band around the dragon's neck. The man ran a hand along the wide metal band as he continued, "You will continue to do my bidding. It will be so for as long as I desire. And you will live in this mountain in solitude until you can be trusted. A dragon with a conscience," he scoffed as he left the cavernous lair.

"Years passed," intoned a narrator. "How long, no one knows for certain. The dragon lay in wait for the sorcerer to return, relegated to the mountainous prison, and doomed to do his bidding by the immovable magic torque around her neck. She was consumed with self loathing, unable to leave the lair, unable to return to her original form, unable to end her miserable life."

"People here are descended of dragons?" I whispered fiercely to Timbra.

"Were," she whispered in return. "No one has seen a dragon in nearly a hundred years. She was the last."

"The people of Thayer rose up in retribution," the narrator continued, as did the play.

"As Edina was trapped in her mountain prison, one by one we hunted and destroyed the remaining dragons who had attacked the stewards of our land. Edina's confinement was also her salvation, for she escaped the revenge.

"Many years later a Thayerian hunting in his wolf form followed a strange scent and discovered Edina. She was listless and ignored him. Drawn to her, and cognizant that she might be the last dragon alive, he visited for months. He slowly trusted that she meant him no harm. She told him of her enslavement, her regret, her despair. He came to care for her, and sought a way to release her from the torque. It took many more months, but the wolf found magic strong enough to remove the sorcerer's powerful claim. When Edina was released, her dragon was replaced by a woman. The wolf took her to his home where he hid her, protected her, and loved her for many, many years.

"The sorcerer never stopped searching for his dragon, and one day discovered the two. Neither Edina nor the wolf were ever seen again. Some say they escaped and started life anew; some say the sorcerer destroyed them both. No one knows for sure."

"We have stories like this where I come from, too," I stage whispered. "They're called 'fairy tales.'"

Timbra's smooth forehead suddenly creased with disapproval. "Everybody knows that fairy tales evolved from real stories, Stella. Even this one has a modest basis in actual occurrences."

"Yeah, but wolf/dragon love? Come on."

"After being in Thayer this long I'd think you could acknowledge that magic exists—that 'unbelievable' is often just due to a prosaic bent in the mind of the beholder."

"Oh! Did you just insult me?"

"You got that?" Timbra smirked.

"Careful, girl. I love you, but that don't mean I won't cut a bitch," I said with mock fury.

The scene of the reenactment changed again, this time to plentiful fields and wagons full of bountiful harvests.

The narrator resumed his soulful delivery once more, "It took a very long time for the surviving Gnome, Fae, and

Dwarf people to repopulate and reclaim their role as stewards of our land. But with time, the pain of loss receded and the numbers within families increased.

"Today we celebrate those noble people whose knowledge and labor provides for us all.

"Today we remember the tragic loss they suffered, that we suffered."

"Today we are reminded that we must always be vigilant, always be mindful that although it has been centuries since that tragic day, the threat remains. Brandubh lives."

A

As evening set in, so many bonfires were lit that the square was nearly alight with their flickering orange glow. I learned quickly that bonfires were a symbolic way to frighten away mischievous spirits, thereby ensuring a good harvest and prosperity. I loved the folklore of the festival, and was happy to know more about the world that had fast become my beloved home.

"Julianne!" I spotted a girl whom I sat next to in lab on the other side of an enchanted kissing booth. She was dressed in a white toga and sported a leafy wreath atop a full head of springy curls. Her cup of womanly bounty runnethed over, and she was having some difficulty keeping the strapless side of her toga PG.

"Hey, girls," she hollered, waving with the hand that was not busy imitating a strap.

Julianne was well proportioned and gorgeous. Her curvy hips swished to and fro as she headed our way. She was one of those people who made you smile the moment you encountered her. Not only was she funny, but she was generous with her own contagious laughter. She was a lot of fun on girls' night because she made keen, if tacky, observations that had me rolling in the floor. Quick-witted and catty? Come sit by me.

"Come to see me sacrificed to the fertility gods, eh?" she asked. "Well, you're too late. I've done my duty and am now in a heat to shed this blasted virginity. Got any recommendations? How about that Adder guy I see hanging around you two? He looks like he swings a big stick."

Timbra choked at the shock of the statement, and I gave Julianne a reprimanding glare. Her mischievous grin told me she knew damn well what she was doing to poor Timbra. Seemed her secret crush was not much of a secret, after all.

"This is my first time," I exclaimed, detouring from the subject of Boone's aptitude. "What's with the get-up?"

"Oh, my family always puts on reenactments of the ancient fertility rituals. We dress in togas and twirl around a fire. It's all very subdued, really."

She narrowed her eyes, debating whether or not to tell us something, then gave a quick nod; she had decided in our favor.

"The authentic stuff, though, takes place tonight. If you're up for it," she finished with a smirk.

"What kind of 'authentic stuff?'" Timbra's womanhood had been challenged. Twice. "Trust me, if you can handle it, we can handle it."

I bugged my eyes at my new BFF. I had no interest in getting involved in hokey rituals in the dark. Not my scene. I could not watch horror movies because they stuck with me for so long afterward. I had no desire to be scared in a theater or my own home; no way was I agreeing to a real-life spook show.

But the two didn't care about my view on the matter, and before I knew it Timbra had signed us up for a full-moon fertility rite that Thayerians had been performing since the dawn of time.

I waved an exasperated goodbye to Julianne, who giggled and bounded away.

"Until midnight, ladies," she called.

"Timbra Redfern! I can't believe you've committed us to this nonsense."

"Well," she complained, "I could hardly turn her down, now could I? '*Swings a big stick*.' Ugh. I shoulda punched her in the giant boob." Her petite ears twitched with irritation.

Timbra pissed was a sight I never thought to see. She rarely uttered an unkind word, and at the boob comment, I lost it and giggled uncontrollably. I continued to giggle until a sight around the corner caught my eye.

It was Gresham, and I wanted to say hello. As we approached I could see he wasn't alone and was, in fact, involved in a heated conversation. I was horrified to eavesdrop, but his deep voice always carried and the two were speaking loudly.

"It's nothing. It's not what you think," Gresham said.

"Oh, I think it's *exactly* what I think," said a woman's voice tinged with bitterness. "I know what I saw, Rowan. Your hands were all over her; your body too close to be innocuous. I'm no fool, not anymore."

"Livia, you're being ridiculous. And this conversation is over. If you don't want to see things that upset you, stop spying on me. Just because you can use scrying to invade my privacy doesn't mean you should."

"Oh, no, this conversation is just getting started. You know what I saw in your future, Rowan. It was her. That…that child! After that little revelation, I'd be a fool not to check up on your private lessons. And I was right."

Timbra and I exchanged a weighted glance. We both knew I was the subject of this conversation. What revelation was she talking about? What future? Also, I was getting damn tired of being called a child.

"That's enough, Livia. Walk away or don't; at this point I'm indifferent to either course of action. But know this—I'll not endure any more of your allegations."

"Indifferent," she gasped. Her tone, previously venomous, was vibrating with pain and outrage. "Well, that's all I need to know, isn't it? Fuck you, Rowan. Fuck you and your *indifference*."

Timbra and I had tried to back away unnoticed to give them what privacy we could. Unfortunately, I tripped on a tent stake and knocked a canister of artisan baby rattles onto a bongo display. Pretty much a worst-case scenario. Livia Miles swung her head in our direction, her eyes widening with fury when they met mine as I lay sprawled among the drums. Sure could've used some premonition about then.

"Oh, that's just bloody perfect," she spat before storming off in a graceful blur.

Gresham stared after her for a long moment, and then turned in our direction after a protracted blink.

"I'm so sorry," I stammered. "We didn't realize you weren't alone until it was too late. I'm sorry if I made things worse."

"You've done nothing wrong, Stella. It's been over between Livia and I for a long time. What you saw was just…the end."

I was too horrified to ask any questions about her 'revelation,' and the extended silence had grown uncomfortable.

"Ah, we're headed to hear Layla Avenatio's band," I blurted. "Want to join?"

"No thanks, girls. I've had enough fun for one night, I think. Enjoy the show. Enjoy yourselves. You've no plans to go down to the riverbank, I hope?"

"Nope," I said at the same time Timbra shrugged noncommittally.

At my questioning look she whispered, "That's where we're meeting Julianne."

"What's at the riverbank, Gresham? Why did you ask?" The whole thing seemed more and more like a very bad idea.

"Oh, no, Stella Stonewall," he laughed, eyes dancing and mouth twitching with mirth. "If you don't know, I'm not telling. This will be quite a baptism into Thayerian culture."

And with that cryptic remark, he walked into the night shaking his head, still laughing at me. I was sure glad I was able to do something to lighten his mood.

A

Layla's band was phenomenal. Shiny Things' sound was haunting and gritty, and Layla's voice was shockingly good. She and four talented band-mates, who were all tattooed, pierced, cinched, and monocled in a steampunk/throwback sideshow freak theme, played to a rapt audience. We had connected with Boone and Ewan, and were sitting contentedly in the grass.

"Ewan?" I asked in as aloof a manner as possible. "You know anything about a midnight rite of passage taking place near the river?"

"Hmm?" he leaned in to me in order to hear over a particularly enthusiastic accordion solo. God, he smelled so good—masculine and woodsy, and faintly of citrus. I leaned in closer and inhaled. He smelled so delicious that the impulse struck me without warning. One minute I thought I'd like to lick his lips as if he'd dipped them in the whipped cream on a cappuccino, and the next minute…I was doing it. I leaned up onto my knees for a better angle, ran one hand behind his back, and the other into the thick hair at the back of his head. I lazily fulfilled my little fantasy before kissing him solidly on the mouth.

I can now admit that I may have been a little drunk from two pints of pear mead. Okay, I was a lot drunk from three pints of pear mead. Whatever. Solstice Fest.

Ewan was so stunned at my actions that he did nothing. Finally—finally!—he reciprocated. With a growl, he ran a thick arm around my middle and threw me onto my back. He braced himself over me, his breaths shuddering in and out as dark hair fell in fat, messy coils around his face. The look in his eyes was so savage that I had a terrifying little moment to decide whether to scream and scramble from his cage, or to throw myself at his beast. I chose the latter. Ewan Bristol kissed me like a drowning man seizing the last precious gulps of air. Fuzzy as my brain had become I was cognizant enough to think, "Now this is passion," just before I couldn't think at all.

I was brought back to my senses by the very loud, very insistent throat clearing of one Timbra Redfern. Breaking free of Ewan took effort, though he still held his body above mine, only our lips touching. He slowly leaned up, allowing me to sit upright on my elbows, the maximum physical effort I was willing to put forth at that particular moment.

"You're going to want to see this," Timbra assured me, shooting for disapproval but failing as she grinned and looked back and forth between me and Ewan.

"See wha…" I began, but trailed off after catching the focus of her attention. Dressed in a burgundy corset with leather trim and brass grommets, a micro mini and fishnets with strategically-placed snags, Layla was a steampunk wet dream. Her bone corset cinched at the back with laces, and around her neck and bust with leather belts. Victorian boots rose to her knees and were obviously vintage.

But all of the careful planning of her wardrobe was grossly overshadowed by the event taking place at that moment, because live on stage Layla was changing into her animal form. As she sang the final note of a particularly haunting number, the band's leather and clockwork-modded instruments straining to compete with the raw power of Layla's voice, she exploded into her crow from the vivid tattoo at her chest.

The crowd gasped as Layla erupted into flight across the amphitheater, her grommeted accoutrements thudding to the floor.

We all sat in stunned silence before realizing that the rest of the band had exited the stage while we consumed Layla's sensational transformation.

A

"Where to now, ladies?" Boone asked. It was hard to imagine topping the evening after Layla's band's display. I invited Boone and Ewan along to meet Julianne, delighted with the idea of two big bodies to serve as protectors.

We made our way to the riverbank, to a well-known spot where a bend in the Basel and some well-placed gravel had formed a "blue hole" of sorts. A rope swing and a wood plank ladder denoted the riverbank as a prime swimming locale. We were the first to arrive, but before long people streamed in. By the time I saw Julianne a crowd of thirty or forty had amassed, some pilfering the woods and riverbank for firewood. They built a big bonfire near the water, its warmth exponentiating the existing June heat.

"You still game, girl?"

Julianne, who had changed into a simple summer dress, appraised Timbra before turning to Boone. "I bet you are, big man."

"You know it," Boone tossed out, earning him the stink eye from Timbra.

"Two minutes to midnight," Julianne yelled, to which the small crowed yipped and whooped. She twisted her blond curls into a loose bun and secured the whole thing together with an elastic.

"Ah, what happens at midnight?" I asked.

Throughout the night, I had come up with a dozen horror-filled scenarios. Not one included us making it out with all of our fingers. I sure didn't expect the next thing out of Julianne's mouth.

"Why, skinny dipping, of course."

With that revelation, she peeled her sundress over her head to expose…well, everything, because she was completely bare underneath. And the carpet matched the platinum drapes.

Upon seeing the horrified look on Timbra's blood-drained face I laughed, hard, at the irony of the situation. Modest, reserved Timbra had gotten us into this whole thing and dragged me along kicking and screaming. She thought it some cloaked and candled ritual, but it was just a little nudity. Well, okay, *a lot* of nudity I noticed as the crowd disrobed en masse. This could not be worse for Timbra, who clasped the top of her robe together when it was only she and I getting ready in our bathroom.

I turned just in time to see the very high, very muscular bottom of one Boone Adder as he bounded into the water. Not far behind was Ewan's refined derriere. While having the perfect amount of muscle definition to dimple each side, he also possessed a heft that peaked just before plummeting down into thick thighs. A real handful.

"Come on in, girls," Boone hollered. "The water's fine."

He didn't have to ask Julianne twice. She jiggled in half a dozen places, trotting confidently to the water's edge before toeing into the shallow water. She took her time, that Julianne, making sure everyone had an opportunity to admire her ample goods. I thought she was fabulous.

Timbra, apparently, not so much. "Can you believe that?" she seethed. "Look, she's going right toward Boone and Ewan."

"Steer clear of those buoys, boys," yelled Timbra.

"Come on," I encouraged, snorting with laughter and hopping one legged as I pulled at my shoes and socks. While I was no nudist, I had promised myself upon entering Thayer that I was going to do this thing 100 percent. As I continued to remove my clothes, Timbra sat motionless.

"What's the holdup?" I asked as I pulled one arm through my sleeve.

"I just don't like my options."

"Do you have options?"

"I do!" She sucked her bottom lip in and fidgeted with her hands.

"All right. What are they?" I asked. It was tough for her. I got that. The least I could do was walk her through her decision.

"One, I can strip and let everyone see me naked."

"Yes. And you won't be alone. Come on, conform!"

"I could also admit that she's beat me; pack it up and go home."

"You could. I hope you won't."

140

"Or I could sit here and have a pity party."

"Come on, Timbra. You can't let her beat you! What's a little nudity among friends?"

She quirked an unimpressed eyebrow at me.

Timbra was a good friend to me. She was good and honest and supportive. I began to put my shirt back on. If she was uncomfortable with our situation, then I should return the support.

"What are you doing?" she asked.

"No way am I leaving you here on the bank alone. If you don't want to go, no big deal. I'll stay with you."

"No. Oh, no, no no." Timbra shook her head and squared her jaw. She threw back her shoulders and took a deep breath.

I gasped in shock, but quickly threw out a "Good girl!" as she ripped her shirt off and threw it to the rocky river bank.

That one action summed up Timbra Redfern entirely. She may never have gotten comfortable with the idea for herself, but for me she put her fear and pride aside without hesitation. In no time we were both down to bra and panties.

I unclasped my lavender bra in record time, slid matching panties down, and stepped free. An arm across my bouncing C's, I dashed into the water and found the cover of the depth much sooner that Julianne had.

"Come on, Timbra," I yelled back to the bank.

She stood where I left her, clad only in bra and panties, her willowy body beautifully illuminated in the orange glow of the bonfire. I could see the moment she made her decision. She stepped forward, moving gracefully toward the water. She entered with her underthings still on, choosing her own fourth option.

Julianne had moved on after Timbra's firelit display, and Boone, Ewan, Timbra, and I gathered in a very spacious circle. The other skinny dippers laughed and splashed around us, some shouting for another beer to their cohorts on the bank. I had not been skinny dipping before, and was shocked to discover how freeing it was to be in the cool water unclothed. The slight currents against skin usually covered was exciting, not in an overtly sexual way, but an 'I'm being naughty and it feels so right' kind of way. I swam away from the others for a bit, enjoying the feel of my long hair flowing behind me as I swam underwater.

After a while, the swimmers slugged out of the water, and Julianne once again took charge.

"All right, ladies. Truth time."

Timbra and I both eyed each other cautiously.

"What now?" I murmured.

At this point of the Midsummer celebration, it was apparently customary for the sexes to separate and I, for one, was glad of that. I was not pleased, however, that we were still naked. This seemed to only be an issue for a select few. Maybe nudity was a Thayerian thing—all the animal instincts and changing forms and whatnot.

As Julianne led us to the edge of the woods, I looked over my shoulder at the men, who had begun jumping over the bonfire, dicks a' danglin'. A more ignorant display of machismo I had never seen.

The girls in the group followed Julianne toward a line of trees lining the bank. The night was so warm that I soon forgot my lack of clothes. I loved the feel of old leaves and spongy earth between my bare toes. The canopy of trees prevented even the moon's filtered light from reaching the forest floor. No one had brought a lantern, but vision in the cover of darkness wasn't a problem. One more benefit of the heightened senses that I'd been experiencing since coming to Thayer. We approached a small clearing, the center of which was occupied by a dilapidated stone well that rose to my waist. The moon's radiance filtered in once again.

"Who's first? No one? Fine, I'll go," Julianne pronounced. With great ceremony she clasped a talisman of some sort to her chest before leaning over the stone structure. Her white bottom shined in the moonlight like a cherub's cheeks as she incanted solemnly.

"This Midsummer eve
When night is fleeting
And the day most long
As the heat of the sun
Impregnates the earth
Fertile, too, my fate make
Upon the water, now, I beg
Reveal the sire of my brood."

"Brood? What's a brood?" I whispered to Timbra.

"Your children," she breathed back.

"Wait. She's asking a wishing well who her baby daddy is gonna be? Is she for real?"

"Incantations are just another form of spellmaking, Stella," she reprimanded. "Used with a talisman, it can be a very accurate form of divining."

When Julianne leaned back up, she grinned like the cat that ate the canary. The other girls giggled with anticipation and asked what she'd seen.

"You know better," she admonished the crowd. "If I want it to come true, I can never tell."

"Bullshit," I said. "This whole thing is nonsense. There's no way to divine your future husband…not from looking into a well at least."

"No?" Julianne raised one eyebrow in challenge. "Then what's the harm?"

"All right." I yanked the talisman from Julianne's outstretched hand, leaned over the well with a huff, and recited the chant with some help.

As I spoke the last word the water began to churn, its surface taking on an opaque and foggy sheen. A figure began to form in the mist. It was broad, powerful. The face began to form and I jerked, backing away from the well and the secrets it held.

"Well," Timbra urged impatiently. "What did you see? Who did you see?"

"Nothing," I said. "No one. I didn't know him."

143

"If you saw nothing, then it can't have been a stranger, Stella. Tell me!"

I shut her down. I didn't want to share; couldn't share. And I didn't believe in that bullshit anyway. My heart beat so fast that I had to force my breaths to slow, to calm down.

"You believe in this crap, don't you?"

"I do," Timbra said defensively. "I'd think you would, too. You say Thayer is your home now, yet you balk at every ritual and history that doesn't conform to your preconceptions. If you're going to be a true Thayerian, you're going to have to leave your old biases behind."

She was right. My first impulse was still to doubt and condemn anything that was new or weird or different. I hated that very habit that had permeated the culture of my small Southern town.

"Your turn." I no longer wanted to focus on me, on my own very long list of flaws.

I couldn't read Timbra's face when she rose from the well, but she found my eyes immediately. She gave Julianne a cool glance and led me back toward the fire.

We found and donned our clothes. Wet, undy-shaped outlines quickly appeared on Timbra's. The boys were ready to head back as well, and we left together, choosing to walk rather than travel by intention.

I had only recently learned that all the cool kids called the magical mode of travel *tracing*. Gresham was certainly not one of the cool kids. I idly wondered what he was doing at the moment, and hoped that he wan't too upset about his break-up with Dean Miles. He didn't seem too affected, but I doubted he would let on in front of me, at any rate.

I was pulled out of my head and into present company by the slip of Ewan's hand around the back of my neck. His warm palm and big fingers grasped me firmly as he stepped in front of me. His eyes intent on mine, he approached me achingly slowly for another kiss.

Just as he neared my lips, his hot breath sliding across my mouth, wild screaming erupted from the group we had just left—desperate, savage screams. Mere moments after those cries, we heard more from the direction of town and turned to see smoke rising from Caliph Square.

"What the hell?" Boone gasped.

After a few uncertain beats, I barked "Boone, Timbra, check the swimmers. Ewan and I'll trace into the square." Everyone gave a sharp nod, and we set off.

I didn't think to hold on to Ewan while tracing, and we obviously *intended* two separate locations because I landed at the square alone. I scoured what little area I could see through the smoke, but quickly abandoned my efforts to find him once I comprehended the fiery chaos that was Caliph Square. Tents were aflame all around me, their taut fabric decimated in seconds, leaving only wooden stakes smoldering in the darkness. Trees and awnings had caught fire, too, sending more suffocating smoke throughout the square. I lifted my shirt over my nose, but breathing was impossible. I needed to get out of the area fast before I lost consciousness. I looked around in search of an escape, and saw that festival-goers were alight and shrieking in agony. I was catatonic with fear.

I couldn't breathe. Couldn't move. Couldn't think. My instincts took over in the absence of conscious thought. Chills skittered up my back in an eerie foreboding, and I ducked just in time to escape the grasp of calloused and knobby talons the size of pit bulls as they clasped madly for my shoulders.

"Dear god," I breathed as three winged nightmares speared through the night. "Dragons."

I stood enthralled with their powerful grace, watching as the force of their fiery breath engulfed rows of festival tents in flame. I stood dumbfounded until that same dragon circled me again, seizing a second opportunity to impale me with those dagger-like talons. Its massive leathery wings "whoofed" in flight with each forceful down thrust. The dragon stretched its scaled neck and roared in fury, sending a column of fire into the sky so hot that the color was a palest green, almost blindingly white to the eye.

When its demented emerald gaze met mine my heart stuttered, and I thought that one of my useless panic attacks was coming on. I soon realized, though, that something else deep within my soul was churning. I sensed that familiar thrumming in my chakra that Gresham had taught me to manipulate. I fanned the flame madly in the nanoseconds before the savage dragon dove at my head once more.

In a flash, my body detonated. There was no graceful leaping or symbiotic transformation. One second I was regular old human Stella Stonewall, and the next I exploded into a huffing, snarling giant red wolf.

I stood stunned for longer than was safe. A wolf! I was a wolf! I had finally found my other form, and it was glorious and powerful and right. I was so pleased with myself; I'd finally done it. I couldn't wait to tell Gresham and the others.

It was odd to stand on four legs, and I was keenly aware of move-able ears and a tail. I was perfectly sentient, and thank god for that because I used my four powerful wolf legs to run like hell toward the river and to propel myself under the nearby bridge. Thick claws helped me crawl right up the stone bridge's steep incline, into a cave-like space between solid ground and the thick abutment of the ancient structure.

The crevice-like space and the width of the bridge ensured that no fire could reach me. I plopped my haunches down, panting, as if it was the most normal thing in the world. And it was. I was at ease in the strange body. My hearing was keen, that was certain, as was my sense of smell. Smoke and the sickening scent of burning flesh were nearly overwhelming. I breathed through my mouth, continuing to pant, to avoid the horrific smells. I was frightened of the dragons and I was horrified and angry that they had likely killed Thayerians and were continuing to do so. What I needed was a plan. I felt guilty hiding out while people were being terrorized and charred just feet from me. But I had no defense against *dragons*. A wolf is scary and vicious, sure, but one snort from a fiery nostril would set my red fur aflame.

As I sat contemplating my next move, another wolf raced under the bridge's overhang and came to a sliding, panting stop to join me in the dark, narrow hiding spot.

I knew that it was Ewan, just by his scent. I wanted to speak to him and had a frustrating little moment to think *'Well, here's one downfall of the form—a communication barrier.'* My head pounded a bit; whether from the smoke or the stress of the change, I wasn't sure. But then Ewan's wolf whined softly and leaned his head away from the chaos of the square. I grasped what he intended. I growled and shook my own head, refusing his encouragement to leave my safe haven and run into the night. At that precise moment, I heard the *whoosh* of a dragon's gnarled plumage, and hot smoke engulfed our hideout and singed my sensitive nostrils.

Unable to reach us, the angry beast tore at the bridge with its powerful talons, threatening to pull my shelter apart piece by piece.

I nodded once to Ewan, and we sprinted from the other side of the covering along the riverbank and into nearby woods.

I ran as far and as fast as my four paws could take me, eventually scrambling up a steep incline and faltering due to my unfamiliarity with the lupine body. Ewan, who had been flanking me and pressing me to go faster, slowed to help me. As I found purchase in the loose layers of fallen leaves, Ewan remained behind me, presumably in case I slipped again. A high-pitched screech pierced the air just behind us. Sheer terror fueled my newfound speed, and I bolted through the heavy underbrush of the forest. I could feel the creature's hot breath through the fur on my back as I ran with every ounce of strength left in my body.

When I reached the face of a small bluff, I spotted a shallow cave entrance and dashed inside. I waited for Ewan, but he never came. I waited and listened, but heard nothing. Whining quietly, I feared the worst. I lay down on the cool, damp floor of the small cave, my hind legs stretched out behind me and my snout resting on my front paws. I didn't know if Ewan had escaped in time or not.

I cursed my new body. I was furious that my incompetence had put his life in danger. I was angry with Ewan for sacrificing himself by lagging behind to protect me. I was mad at myself because here I sat once again helpless and waiting for someone else to save me. Finally, I was incensed at Gresham because I had no idea how to return to my human form. In weeks of training, not once had we covered that precious bit of material.

Whoop...whoop...whoop. Gnarled wings the size of Volkswagens blew rocks and dust around my tiny cave like a personal sandstorm.

Still rigid with anger, and so suddenly overwhelmed with a fear that ran bone-deep, the sacred place within my chest pulsed again.

No, I thought frantically. *Not back to human now. I might as well bite into an apple and serve myself up to the prehistoric beast.*

I was so *sick* of being helpless, of being ignorant about my body, my form, and my parentage. I was mad as hell, and I wasn't going to take it anymore. I spotted a sharply-filed stick that a previous camper had left in the cave, and planned to use it for a weapon once I turned.

I had one final fleeting thought. *Dragons be damned; I'm gonna fight,* before my body exploded once more.

Something hurt. It was my head. And there was an immense pressure on my back. I was trapped, in what I didn't know. I threw my arms out in an effort to free myself. Except...those weren't arms. I craned my head to gain a better look at first one side of my body and then the other. *Whatthehell?* I was so confused. I couldn't comprehend what I was seeing. My mind refused to deal with my reality, and began to shut down. I was lightheaded. My vision became cloudy, and

tiny white stars floated across my line of sight. I flailed my
body to catch myself before I fell. When I did, I burst out of
the cliff-side cave and defaced the entrance dislodging boulders
and causing an avalanche of smaller rocks and dust until the
cavity was unrecognizable. Still unstable and erratic I turned in
a circle but listed clumsily to the right. My balance was way out
of whack. As I turned, my large tail whipped saplings into
projectile splinters. *Tail? I had a tail!* A scaly, powerful,
beautifully fearsome tail. My body began to wrack with
shudders, a physical response to the mental shock I was
undergoing. I could feel the vibrations of my shudders in my
arms. No, not arms. Wings.

I was in a dream. My mind had become so overwhelmed
that it had given up. Nothing made sense, but it didn't matter.
It wasn't real. Conscious fear and doubt were suspended. I
embraced the moment, carefully extended each wing, awed by
the sheer power the two held. Rusty auburn in color, thick but
pliable leathery skin was stretched taut between long bones that
were previously my fingers. A strange little claw extended
about midway along the top and I wiggled it. *My thumb. Still
opposable!*

Any further exploration of my bitchin' new body was cut
short as the dragon that had been tormenting me dove down
once more and screeched in warning.

I was a dragon. I was a dragon! I was fierce and
powerful…and still quite pissed. I gave a menacing screech in
return. My attacker wasn't expecting to encounter another
dragon, and when realization dawned, it flexed massive wings
in the opposite direction, retreating back into the night with
one last bewildered look over its shoulder.

I was pleased with myself and raised an arm in victory,
thinking *Yee-yah!* The result, much to the forest's misfortune,
was another felled sapling and a small canopy fire that luckily
fizzled out soon enough.

*O*nce the threat of being dragon bait was gone, I was at a loss of what to do next. I didn't know how to revert to my human body. I sure as hell didn't know how to fly. I did try, but after several failed attempts to manipulate my new body, cognitive thought returned and I remembered that I could trace. It probably worked even in my animal form— wouldn't hurt to try. There was only one place I knew to go for help: Gresham's.

I picked up a scaly, clawed foot, tried not to dwell too long on that, and then crashed heavily into Gresham's back yard. I decimated an ornamental tree and yards of plush sod. In mere seconds, Gresham charged through the French doors swinging a...*was that a claymore?*

I sat very still, ensuring that he knew I would not attack. He stopped just short of me, mouth agape and eyes wide before hoarsely croaking, "Stella?" He put down the oversized sword and paced around my big body, taking every inch of me in. He ran a hand along my shiny bronze scales.

"Beautiful. Just beautiful," he breathed. "I knew it."

I huffed through my nostrils in pleasure at his compliment.

Wait, what? This was news. Surely he didn't mean that he knew my form was a dragon. And if so, I had news for him; I was a wolf, too. Which reminded me of the whole set of questions I had relating to *that* fact. How could I have two forms? How was it even possible, considering what I knew of animal forms, which was that they were a genetic heritage and two different species couldn't produce offspring.

I must have begun to look agitated—I *was* agitated because I couldn't communicate these questions to him.

Gresham stepped back slowly, murmuring "Easy now." I made an effort to relax and he released a breath.

"I assume you'd like to return to your original form?" he asked, to which I blinked a coarse eyelid.

"All right then. I suppose we should have covered this material, but I never thought you would change without me."

Another, longer blink.

"Compared to what you've done tonight this is the easy part. Just relax."

I quirked an eyebrow at him. I mean, *really*. How many relaxed dragons had he seen?

"Okay, maybe you'll not achieve 'relaxed' tonight, but how about…concentrate."

That I could do.

"Good girl. Now, focus on your chakra. Do you have it?"

Blink.

"Good. Picture yourself as human once more. Imagine looking into your chakra as if it were a mirror and seeing your long hair, smooth skin. Picture the sprinkling of freckles just across your nose. Imagine your arms ending in fingers and your long legs into narrow feet. Can you see it? Can you see even that freakishly tiny pinkie toe?"

I *could* see it. And then I was shrinking. I folded in on myself again and again. It wasn't painful; just a constant pressure and the ultimate sense of weird. The entire process lasted maybe ten seconds, and once it was finished I lie on my side on the ground naked, breaths ragged and chest heaving.

Gresham shed his white button down shirt and threw it around me, scooping me up into his arms. He smoothed my wild hair again and again and murmured words of soothing encouragement until my breathing slowed. I looked up at him.

"I bet you have a lot of questions," he said.

I sure did. I blinked my agreement, still unable to produce the effort to speak, and he gathered me tighter into his arms and carried me to the kitchen banquette before putting a kettle on the gas burner.

"I'll be right back with something to cover you," he said before bounding up the stairs.

I sat in the familiar corner of his kitchen, my mind gone numb with shock and confusion. I had so many questions that I didn't know where to start. Even asking questions seemed too great an effort. I wanted to lie down, to close my eyes for just a moment. 'Dealing' was out of the question.

I heard a noise in the hallway and assumed it was Gresham. My head bowed as I struggled to stay awake.

"Well, that didn't take long, did it?" Her strained voice was high pitched with emotion.

Dean Miles. *Shit.*

"I knew it. I saw you in his bed in my divination. No one knows better than me how smooth he is, but I never thought he would work this fast."

I was aware of how the situation looked. My hair was disheveled and I had on nothing but Gresham's unbuttoned white shirt. My knees were drawn up to my chest seeking comfort and I was probably showing a teeny bit of ass.

"Dean Miles, it's not what you think…" I began tiredly, but was cut off by her sharp bark of laughter.

"Oh, don't give me that shit. If you're woman enough to fuck my man, surely you're woman enough to own up to it."

Well, that was just rude. In fact, she had always been rude to me. As a teacher, a mentor, I should have been able to count on her for guidance. To trust her. But she treated me like an ignorant nuisance since the moment she laid eyes on me. And she'd insulted me so many times that I'd lost track. "Why, *Livia*, you're forgetting one very important thing," I said in feigned innocence. "He's no longer your man."

Her head snapped up, her nostrils flared, and she sprinted toward me. Despite my exhaustion, I welcomed her attack. I relished the thought of getting my hands around her bony neck. I smiled and braced my legs for a fight.

Gresham stepped down from the stairs as she neared me, blocking her path. He started at seeing her, but recovered and threw the robe he was carrying to the side. He'd become the focus of her fury.

"You bastard," she grated. "After all this time together I find her here, like this, mere hours after we end it? You disgust me. I told you, did I not? I warned you I saw her in your bed. And here she is." Her hands shook and her lip trembled. She was on the verge of completely losing it.

"Yes, you told me, Livia," Gresham said evenly. "Do you need something?"

"Do I need something?" she repeated. "Do I *need* something? I came to apologize, to say maybe I had spoken in haste. But it's glaringly obvious I was right."

She turned to me with a snarl, "You'll pay for this, little girl."

"That's enough, Livia," Gresham said. "Stella's done nothing wrong. Remember your position at Radix. There's no need for retribution. You and I are through."

"Remember my position? You mean that I'm her teacher? That you're fucking my student? How could I forget something like that?"

She turned and left without another word, slamming the front door behind her.

The teapot whistled, drawing our gazes away from the door.

"Tea's ready," Gresham said dryly.

A

"Why did you let her believe we were sleeping together?" I asked Gresham as he poured steaming water over tea in first my, and then his own, cup.

"She saw what she wanted to see. There was no convincing her otherwise—not tonight. Trying to make her see the truth would only have escalated the argument."

"Do you want me to say something to her once she's had a chance to cool down? Clear things up? I hate to come between you."

"No. I'll tell her in time. Truthfully, our relationship lasted longer than was good for anyone."

I didn't know what to say to that. On some level, I was glad he no longer wanted Dean Miles. I felt a shameful thrill knowing they had fizzled out; that he didn't care if she thought we'd been intimate. I didn't want Gresham to myself, but deep down I didn't want the evil professor to have him, either.

"I really just wanted to get her out of the house as quickly as possible. She's a sharp tongue, and I imagine a heated argument is the last thing you'd like to have right now?"

I shrugged.

"I am sorry she insulted you. And she'll likely hold a grudge. I hadn't thought that part through, I'm afraid, until it was too late."

"Eh. I'll survive. What, will my parents be disappointed if I get a C?"

Wait a minute. My parents, I thought. "Gresham, there's something I need to tell you."

"Hmmm?"

"You saw my dragon tonight, but what you didn't see was….well…I turned into a wolf first."

I relayed the night's events to him, including Ewan's disappearance.

"I'd just come back from the square when you arrived," he said. "A lot of damage. Luckily, we were able to treat those who were burned. I've heard some speculation as to why the dragons attacked, and I tend to agree with it."

"What have you heard?" I asked.

"It's believed the attack on Caliph Square was carried out by the same man who sought to annihilate the Gnome and Fae races centuries ago."

"The one from the play? The one who used dragons?"

Gresham nodded somberly. "The same. His name is Brandubh; he is an extremely powerful and dangerous wizard. He's also raving mad."

"What kind of name is Brandoo. Is that a last name?"

"Brandubh means 'black raven.' His actual name is Typhoen and, more than a powerful wizard, he is rumored to have been an ancient god, the 'father of all monsters.' No one really believes that, but Brandubh certainly never discouraged the rumor. Fear, respect, it's all the same to him."

"Where did you get all of this information?" I asked.

"I have my sources," he said with a smirk.

"I thought the dragons were gone."

"So did I" he replied, his tone clipped in ager, his posture rigid.

"Well, what does Brandubh want now? And why burn down the town?"

"I think it's likely they were searching for you, Stella, and for the very thing you discovered tonight. I think they came in search of another dragon."

"But how would Brandubh know I even exist, especially when I didn't know myself?"

"Brandubh is a well-known clairvoyant. He probably saw the moment you entered Thayer. Dammit." He rose and began pacing. I've put you in danger and for that I'm sorry."

I could only shake my head. "How would they know to look for me at the festival?

"An educated guess. Everyone goes. Once you left the protective wards of Radix you were fair game."

"Wait a minute, Gresham." My ears rang as I began to put the many clues I'd gathered together. I had an awful suspicion. "If Brandubh knew to look for me due to a vision, how did *you* find me?"

A

Gresham grudgingly told me the rest of the story, revealing details that I'd been seeking for weeks. He said the legend of the Steward Massacre was true; that the dragon Edina and her wolf lover were real.

When Brandubh discovered the two in hiding he sought to destroy them both. But the clever wolf acted as a decoy while a pregnant Edina escaped. In a vicious battle, Brandubh fatally injured the wolf. Someone found the dying wolf in the woods and tried to save him. In tortured delirium and once again in human form, he ranted over and over, "Run, Edina! Our babe. Save the babe."

The man died that night in the stranger's home and was later given a meager burial, his identity unknown.

The stranger, a Gnome, recognized the unusual name 'Edina,' and didn't discount the man's wild ramblings. The gnome confided in his longtime friend. He suspected the dead wolf and his beloved Edina were the very ones immortalized in the Steward Massacre story. If there was a child…well…that had best be discovered right away, although discreetly.

The gnome's friend and confidante? Rowan Gresham.

Gresham searched more than twenty years, but never turned up a single lead. That is until I came of the age eligible to enter Radix. Livia Miles saw me in her scried divinations. At first it was only a competitor for Gresham's affections that she saw—a faint vision of a redhead in Gresham's life. But other visions soon revealed my name, and my skin morphing into shimmering scales. Livia recounted her visions to Gresham, though he'd never revealed his own knowledge to her.

Gresham searched Thayer futilely before a detail of Livia's vision—a vintage Mustang—indicated my existence outside the confines of Thayer. Gresham pinpointed my location through an Internet search of my name, of all things. He found me, of course, the day he crashed his Land Rover into my beloved Beast.

It was my turn to pace the floor, the angered energy flowing through me too wildly to sit still. "So, all this time you've suspected that my form was a dragon, Gresham? All the confusion and disappointment I've suffered, and you *knew*?"

"No," he shook his head and reached out to touch my arm. "I didn't *know*. Did I suspect? Yes. But the only things Livia's visions revealed were a redheaded Stella Stonewall and scales. Her visions come in fragments, and I'd pieced so many things together. You could have turned into a python, for all I knew. I had to be sure. And the natural course was to allow you to change form without bias."

"Still, why wouldn't you have told me your suspicions? I'm typically pretty reasonable, though I'm not feeling reasonable right now." My teeth had been clenched so long that my jaws began to ache. "I'd think some warning before I turned into *a dragon* would be super helpful to a novice like me."

He ran his hands behind his head and pulled at the hair at the back of his neck. "If I had told you that you were the offspring of a dragon responsible for the attempted genocide of three separate races of people and her wolf lover, would you have believed that?"

"Probably not. But the point is you kept information from me. Whether I believed it or not should've been my choice." I stalked to the table. Took a sip of my tea to dispel the nervous energy.

Gresham's breath came hard through his nose in frustration. "Besides, you're not just a dragon. You're also a wolf, which is beyond comprehension by modern standards. The repercussions of a discovery such as this could be momentous. Are you the only offspring of two such varying species? Can the results be recreated? Are there others like you out there? Or are you something even more unlikely?"

"Like what? What's more unlikely than a wolf-dragon hybrid?"

"What? Well, I can think of one other scenario, but it's less likely even than this one."

I took a deep breath that came back out in a shudder. The more he talked, the smaller I felt. It was as if the universe held me in its palm and I was a dust particle in its infinite hand. I saw my life becoming a study in procreation and genetic genesis.

Once again I began to question what exactly Gresham's interest was in me.

"Stella, are you all right?" Gresham searched my gaze, which had narrowed at him amidst my suspicions.

I could only grunt in his direction.

At once, my addled brain pieced together what Gresham had been saying, a concept that was so foreign, the antithesis of what I knew to be true, that the two things were wholly incongruous.

"My god." I sat down on the banquette, unable to stand a minute more. "Are you saying that my mother is…not just Thayerian, but Edina, the dragon from the massacre?"

My conscious mind was having a hard enough time accepting that I turned into a wolf, then a freaking dragon. My own mother was possibly the villain in a murderous fable? I closed my eyes, held onto the table, concentrating on breathing in and out through my mouth in an effort to avoid fainting.

"She must be," Gresham said. "Besides adoption, there's no other explanation."

"Adoption," I repeated blankly. "No. No. I wasn't adopted. I know it."

"I think it's time you go back to your mother, Stella. Armed with this knowledge, she must understand you need information to protect yourself. If what we suspect is true, there's much that only she knows."

"You're right. I have to know. I'll go tomorrow."

"Would you like me to come? Are you afraid of her?"

"Of my mother? No, Gresham. She's harmless. Gentle. There's no way she's Edina. There must be another explanation, and this is a conversation best had alone." The weight of the world seemed to set on my shoulders at that moment. "I'm tired, Gresham. I have a million questions, but I can hardly keep my eyes open. I wanna go to my room."

"Of course," he said, collecting my teacup and helping me up. He let his arms fall, but kept them around my waist. "I think you're doing exceptionally well absorbing and dealing with this news." His gaze once again held pride.

I smiled weakly and traced from his arms to my room at Sabre Hall.

I woke with a start, my unconscious brain having concluded that I didn't know Boone and Timbra's fate. Since I'd separated from them after the skinny dipping incident, which seemed like a lifetime ago, I had no idea if they'd gotten out of there. I remembered with revulsion the screams coming from the water, the square.

Ewan and I had gone toward the square. Ewan. If Timbra and Boone were okay, they certainly wouldn't be after I shared the tragic news of his disappearance. We'd need to organize a search. Was it even safe for me to go out there? Any of us? Safe or not, I knew we'd do it to find him.

Still clad in Gresham's shirt, I drug my feet into Timbra's room through our adjoining bathroom.

A sharp gasp and an emphatic "Oh, shit" alerted me to the room's occupation. Two naked bodies snatched at sheets and blankets to cover themselves though, really, I had already seen it all. The speed of sight beats reaction time without fail. Unfortunately.

"Stella, thank the gods," Timbra nearly laughed with relief while holding a sheet close to her chest.

"Ahhh. I'm so sorry," I sputtered. "I came to check that you were safe after last night. I didn't…I didn't know. I'll let you two get dressed."

"No. Stay."

At this, Boone whipped his head around to determine her meaning.

"Well, I didn't mean *stay*, obviously. Just….okay," she conceded. "We'll hurry and dress, but don't leave your room. Ewan said you were separated in the woods and he was worried sick you'd been eaten by the dragon that chased you. I want to hear…"

I cut her off. "Ewan? Ewan's *alive?*"

"Of course. What did you think? When everyone discovered what was happening in the square, they traced back to The Root and its impenetrable wards. We all met back up here at Sabre to wait out the attack."

"Uh, ladies?" This from Boone.

"Just a minute." I looked back to Timbra. "So when Ewan disappeared in the woods, he traced back here and you guys, what, hung at the bar all night?"

"Basically, yeah. Why didn't you just trace? Congrats on finding your she-wolf, by the way."

"Guys?" Boone again.

"Thanks. Why didn't I trace?" I trailed off. "Why *didn't* I trace? It never once entered my mind."

I stood in stunned silence, contemplating my idiocy until Boone cleared his throat loudly.

"Hmm?" I said absently.

"Still naked here."

And so he was. I backed through the door from which I had come, and walked back to my bed.

Tracing, I thought. *Of course.*

Surely Ewan discovered that I hadn't traced back to Radix, and came to the bridge to save me. With both of us in wolf form, communicating 'Damn, Stella, trace already' would have been difficult. I was grateful to Ewan for putting his life at risk for mine, but I was also a little peeved that he'd traced back to

The Root, effectively abandoning me to my fate against a dragon.

A

I took a really long shower, which is where I do my best thinking. While shaving my legs I came to terms as best I could with the fact I was now Triple Threat Stella Stonewall: one part brainy redhead, one part vicious red wolf, and one part fire breathing dragon. No big.

Honestly, I was just pleased I'd finally found my form. Okay, so I had two and that was apparently pretty uncommon. Then again, I had never been normal, so nothing new there.

And, okay, so there was an evil sorcerer out to get me because I was a freak of even Thayerian nature. But as long as I stayed inside the boundaries of The Root, I was safe. That was something at least.

I thought I would probably keep the whole *triple threat* thing to myself for a while. No one had seen my dragon besides Gresham. Well, and the attack dragon. Shit. And speaking of attack dragons, I wondered where those had come from if all but my mother had been exterminated hundreds of years ago. Even Gresham didn't know that.

My own problems shelved for the moment, my mind wandered to Boone and Timbra. How did that happen? I couldn't wait to tease Ms. 'What's The Point Unless We Have a Future.' For all her prudish grandstanding, she sure didn't waste any time getting busy like the rest of us.

Rest of *us,* hell. Aside from a little flirting with Gresham and Ewan's kiss, I was the only one suffering through celibacy.

I I knocked tentatively on the dark green door of the simple brick house. I don't know why. I couldn't think of another time…ever…that I had knocked at my own front door. Maybe because I was supposed to be in South Africa. More likely it was because I'd use any excuse to delay this conversation even for a few moments.

I pulled at the dead fronds on a neglected fern as I waited for my mother to answer the door.

I saw her magnified green eye through the peephole, then she opened the door with a flourish.

"Stella, baby. What're you doing here?"

"Oh, just a surprise visit, Mom." I tried to smile, but only succeeded in pulling my lips back in a weird grimace.

"From South Africa?" she breathed, and threw both arms around my neck. She smelled of the subtle moisturizer she applied each morning. I'd forgotten how much taller I was. She was so petite, so delicate. "I thought you couldn't come until the end of the year. But I'm so glad you're here. Come in, come in. Where are your things?" She poked her head out the door and looked around for a car. "How did you get here?"

Ignoring her questions, I made my way inside to the kitchen and found my usual seat at the breakfast bar.

She stood with a hip against the old ceramic sink and looked at me expectantly. "So, tell me everything."

I couldn't meet her gaze. I focused on a scratch on the Formica counter and blurted before I lost my nerve, "I haven't been in South Africa, Mom. I traced here. From Thayer."

I did look at her then. I didn't want to miss the widening of her eyes in surprise, no matter how subtle. She was good. If I hadn't been looking for an indication of her recognition, I would've missed it.

"I can see that you know what I'm talking about, Mother. It's time you told me the truth."

All the color left her face and she went ashen with shock. She opened her mouth to speak, closed it, opened it again, and collapsed to the floor, her eyes rolling back in her head as she went unconscious.

I rushed to her side and cradled her head in my lap.

"Mom. Mom, wake up!" I patted her face gently at first and then harder. I shook her shoulders and pulled strands of dull red hair from her face. What had I done? I should have known she couldn't handle such a shock. I knew she generally only held on by a thread. My stomach roiled with guilt at my abrupt and ruthless questioning.

Her head and hands began to move, and after a few tense moments she came to. She was groggy, but met my gaze and then, maybe recalling the revelation I'd just made, she closed her eyes again and exhaled shakily. I helped her sit upright and we both sat there in silence for several moments. I was giving her time to recover before I pursued the topic again, and she, I assumed, was determining how much to tell me. Finally she rose to her feet and grasped the counter, as if it was the only thing keeping her upright.

"Mom," I began but she stopped me.

"Stella, I can't," she whispered. "I just can't re-open those old wounds without bleeding out entirely. I fought so hard for so long to put the horror, the tragedy, the guilt behind me."

"I know, Mom, and I'm sorry." My lips quivered with emotion at her admission. I sniffed, steeled myself, and pushed ahead. There's so much I need to know. I turned into a dragon, Mom. And a wolf! I need help understanding all of this…I need to know who I am. Why won't you help me?"

"I'm sorry I'm not stronger for you."

"Don't say that; just *be* stronger," I said, beginning to lose my temper. "All I'm asking is for a conversation about my father, about your lineage, about my own. I need to know this. We don't have to discuss your imprisonment."

She began to cry, but I wouldn't let her tears deter me this time. She covered her face with her hands and shook her head over and over. I could no longer see her eyes, but her stooped posture told me she was so upset that she was near grieving. I pushed anyway.

"It's like you're abandoning me and forcing me to fend for myself when I don't even have to. Ignoring this won't make it go away, Mother. You're being…you're being obtuse. Worse, you're being a shitty mother."

I was angry. I knew better than to berate her like that. She was so fragile, so emotionally unstable. But to continue to refuse me information was akin to risking my life.

She removed her hands and looked at me, her pale face stricken at my words and streaked with tears and ruined makeup.

"I'm sorry," I said. "I shouldn't have said that. I just don't understand why you won't help me.

She turned her head and closed her eyes. Her lips trembled, and the rest of her body shuddered, too.

I gritted my teeth and stormed into my room before I said something even more hurtful, slamming the door shut behind me. I sat in my desk chair and shook my head over and again, infuriated and beyond baffled at her continued obstinance.

I took in the little treasures and trophies that littered my room. My normal life, activities like softball and the weekend theater had once meant so much to me. Now I had left them all behind. I felt sad at the thought of abandoning everything I'd known, but wasn't regretful. I was happy to have found my new life, these new parts of myself. Navigating Thayer alone had been difficult and clumsy, but I had done it. If my mother wouldn't, or couldn't, talk about it, then I 'd have to live with it for now. I resolved to continue down the overgrown path that I'd begun clearing one machete swipe at a time. I rose, intending to tell Mom that she needn't worry about more questions from me.

"Mom?" I called out. No sign of her in the kitchen.

"Mom?" I checked the living room and the hall bathroom, but she was neither place. More troubling, she wasn't answering me.

"Mom?"

I pushed open the door to her bedroom. She wasn't there. I noticed that, as usual, her bed was meticulously made; hospital corners snapped and tucked tight.

I searched the entire house, but she was nowhere to be found. I called outside, and she didn't answer; she never returned.

Eventually I went back into her bedroom to she'd packed a bag; if she planned to come back anytime soon. I opened the drawers of her dresser and found everything as it always had been—folded neatly and stored with a bewildering attention to detail.

Confused, angry, and very much afraid, I slammed the dresser drawer shut, rocking the furniture. As I did, an envelope I hadn't seen before fell from its propped position against the mirror. I found my name scrawled hastily across the front. Inside was a short, hand-written note.

My Precious Stella,

I just can't. I can't reopen those old wounds. I can't revisit that time in my life and maintain my sanity. I know this. You were a miracle. A new beginning. Because of you, baby, I sought and found salvation. I love you so much. I leave you with this, and it's as important as anything else I can tell you. You, Stella Stonewall, can achieve anything you desire. The worlds are yours. I'm sorry you must do it alone, but believe me when I say you're better off without something like me guiding your way.

Goodbye Stella. I love you.

Mom

Gone. My mother was gone.

I waited for hours, but had little faith she would return. Ever. Deep down I knew my mother had abandoned me to my confusion and desperate need for information. Rather than talk to me about who I was, who she was, she left me.

I was overcome with grief, and not just for myself, but for my mother—for the unfathomable pain that she must've been in to take such an action. I knew she loved me, knew it without a shadow of doubt.

But love wasn't enough to overcome the deep-rooted pain and fear that I had glimpsed through her vellum-thin shields over the years. I knew she excessively clung to religion. I knew she was, in many ways, a shell of a person. And I knew she had a weak constitution. But I never, for one minute, thought she'd go that far.

I struggled for comprehension and acceptance, but it never came. My shock and grief morphed into anger. The longer I thought and the more time that passed, the angrier I became. I couldn't grasp how she had done this *cowardly* thing, leaving me alone in the world. Tucking her tail and running rather than face her past, rather than tell me the truth about who I was. I was bewildered and supremely disappointed. No, not disappointed. Furious was a better word. I was *furious* with her. Worse, I felt guilty that I was angry with her, and that made me even madder. I'd done nothing to deserve any of this. I was just a child born of love, if I was to believe the legend. A child taken to a new place for a new start. At least there I'd had a loving, protective mother. Now I was in a strange new world with a thousand questions, a volatile body and spirit, and not a single person to whom I could turn or learn the truth behind my mother's horrific actions.

Dammit! I didn't know what to do next. I thought I should probably call the police and report her missing, though the note proved she'd left on her own. The police would surely ask me to what kind of 'old wounds' she was referring. And 'the worlds are yours.' That reference would make her seem unstable. I didn't want all of her friends and neighbors to think she'd lost it and taken off...even though that's precisely what had happened.

A

The police arrived, and I recounted the day's events to them as best I could without revealing any details about, you know, an alternate universe. I gave them my mother's letter, and claimed ignorance at her strange wording and ominous references.

"So, you have no idea what she's talkin' about when she says," Officer Steves looked down at the letter over black-rimmed readers before directing his beady glare at me, "'I cannot reopen those old wounds...'?"

"Well, sir," I said weakly, "I'd been asking her about my father. But I'd been asking the same questions for years."

"Mmph," he grunted, and his gut bounced in concurrence. "No idea where she might've run off to?"

That question I could answer honestly. "No. No idea. We've no family; it's always been just us."

"You've been away at college these last few years. Any new friends she might have made? Any...boyfriends?" he peeked above the readers to note my reaction.

"Not that I know of, no, sir. She spent a lot of time at church. You might talk to the people there."

"Oh, I will. I will. My deputies and I are going to take a look around the place now, if that's all right, and then we'll talk to your neighbors, too."

"Sure. Let me know if I can do anything else."

A

The next couple of days dragged on painfully as my mom's friends and neighbors brought casseroles and brownies, and then escaped as soon as was prudent. The situation made people uncomfortable, and for good reason.

Officer Steves returned to report that Mom had called her pastor and a neighbor to tell them she was leaving indefinitely. She didn't elaborate. He assured me the police department would 'monitor the situation,' but that if she chose to leave town there was no need to investigate any further. I agreed with him. I knew that, unless she wanted them to, no one would ever find her anyway. She had escaped the powerful Brandubh before, after all. She knew how to disappear.

My college roommate, Lizzie, came by, as did a few old friends. But it was when I returned to Thayer—to my friends from The Root—that I felt normal again. It was amazing the connection I had formed with them over the course of several weeks. It was with them that I was most at home, that I felt right. No one asked me questions or expected details or entertainment. They were content to lend support simply with their presence.

I had gathered with friends at Sabre Bar. When I asked Gresham to join us he declined, citing an unwillingness to fraternize with students. I reminded him that he wasn't a professor, and not held to such standards, and he finally relented.

He'd been visibly angered at my mother's disappearance. His reaction shocked me—I thought he was as furious with her as I was. He asked about the circumstances of her disappearance, details. But there was nothing more to tell.

We found our cozy corner and sat comfortably, if quietly at first, in the bar's over-sized chairs surrounding a low table. The addition of Gresham to my group of friends changed the dynamic a bit. He was so overtly guarded and rigid that the group stayed on edge rather than relax into the companionable conversation we typically found.

After a tense few moments Gresham spoke to Timbra, who sat nearest him.

"How's your father, Ms. Redfern? I haven't seen him since a council meeting last fall. He's well, I hope."

"Oh, you know my father. He's tough as a goat and just as stubborn."

Gresham laughed and Timbra jumped at the unexpected sound before bugging her eyes in my direction. I knew the feeling. That laugh was disarming.

"I know it for a fact," Gresham continued. "I assume he's still fighting the new agricultural requirements."

"He is," Timbra nodded with a smile. I stopped following the conversation at that point, though I did wonder about Gresham's involvement in politics. I supposed someone who'd been around for as long as he had probably had a hand in all sorts of pies.

"Boone, how has your metamorphosis been so far?" Gresham asked a bit later. It looked as if he knew he was the odd man out, and was attempting to make nice with my friends.

"Fucking great so far, sir. Oh, shit. Excuse my language. Shit! I did it again. I'm sorry, sir."

Gresham's eyes squinted with amusement, but he was successful in repressing an outright laugh. "No problem," he said. "Just don't call me sir, for gods' sake."

"Dumbass," Layla taunted Boone from the side of her mouth.

"I can't help it," Boone, who was usually grossly over-confident, whined. "He makes me nervous."

The gathering of friends had done the trick. I was less distraught about my mother and comforted by my friends. Or maybe I was just distracted by watching Gresham attempt to smooth out the rumpled dynamic that his presence created. The whole scene was fascinating. Gresham was attempting small talk, Boone was agitated and off his game, Bex flirted with Gresham, who ignored her advances. Ewan, no stranger to introspection, was even more brooding.

I watched him for several moments as he stared at Gresham, his jaw tight. He pushed his hands through his dark curls before turning sharply in my direction. He held my gaze for several moments, determination flooding his keen eyes.

"What exactly is your interest in Stella, Mr. Gresham?" Ewan's blunt question extinguished any other conversation at the table. Ewan forced his gaze from mine and swung menacingly toward Gresham, whose affable smile turned to one better described as 'chilling.'

"My interest? My interests are my own business."

"Usually, I would agree with you. But if your interests involve Stella, then they're my business, too."

I sputtered, taken aback by Ewan's assertion. I blinked three or four times as I tried to understand his statement, his gall.

"Ewan, what the hell?" I finally found my voice at the same time Gresham responded.

"It seems the lady disagrees," Gresham said, turning his predatory smile in my direction.

I shivered. I couldn't tell if they were the turned-on kind of shivers, or the creeped-out kind. Maybe both. I cleared my throat and attempted to clear my mind. When I lifted my eyes from my lap, I found Ewan looking at me as if I'd stomped his baby rabbit. Shock, betrayal, and pain flicked across his features before they hardened. He took a long swig of his dark beer, finishing off the pint and setting it down onto the table much too forcefully. His nostrils flared as he took several breaths and struggled to regain his composure.

The night was going to shit fast.

With someone else in the hot seat, Boone found his confidence once more and facilitated a change of subject.

"These sure are interesting paintings," he said. "You know anything about this artwork, sir...ah, Mr. Gresham?"

"Just Gresham, please, Boone. I do know something about that one there." He indicated a small oil painting near the corner of the room. "If I'm not mistaken, that one is a portrait of a previous vice chancellor..."

Boone and Layla carried on small talk with Gresham. The group eventually grew used to his presence and Ewan's shit mood and picked up scattered conversation. While the occasion was still too serious for the usual fun, we did enjoy a different kind of rapport, a deeper one.

It was as if we'd met the final threshold for becoming true friends. Together we had first experienced a significant rite of passage: our introduction into supernatural higher education. Next we shared the common ambition and ensuing life-altering experience of finding our animal forms. Now my friends commiserated with me as I suffered a confusing loss.

The hole in my heart that my mother's abandonment had carved was still gaping, but thanks to my friends, the edges weren't quite so jagged.

A

"Have any more details surfaced about the attack on Caliph Square?" I asked a bit later. Since I'd been out of town I had yet to discuss the night of the attack with them. "Has anyone heard a final count of people injured or killed?"

"I heard no one actually died, though there were some fairly serious burns," Layla said. "And a lot of torched tents."

"The whole thing is so mysterious," said Timbra.

"I thought there were no more dragons," Boone said. "Where did they come from? And what did they want?"

"Fucking dragons," Ewan spat. "They're evil. They don't need a reason to attack innocent people."

Gresham shot me a weighted glance. He still suspected I was the target. I gathered that the authorities who'd told Gresham they suspected Brandubh were not making that common knowledge. Just as well. It would only serve to terrorize people further, and since there was no proof yet, I could see no need.

Ewan's vehement loathing of dragons hurt me. I knew most people feared and hated dragons. I could understand why. But with the knowledge that I was one...well...being on the receiving end of such blind hatred cut to the core. It also scared me.

I was emotionally spent, and I stood to bid everyone goodnight.

"Thank you all, again, for your support. I felt your love tonight, and I want you to know that I feel the same."

Without warning, Bex hugged me, her lithe arms wrapped around my shoulders. It was so out of character that I let her hug me for a while. She pulled back stiffly and left without another word.

"It'll get easier with time, doll," Layla said and gave me an encouraging pat on the back.

I nodded and started to respond, but Boone wrapped me into his big body and squeezed so tightly I wheezed. I allowed myself to droop just for a minute and enjoy the firm support.

As Boone ambled away I felt the tension radiating from Gresham and Ewan, who were standing behind me.

I turned to see Ewan look to Gresham, who stared back. Their expressions were tight, menacing; their posture awkward. They were sure doing a bang-up job of making the night about their machismo instead of my despair. Jackasses.

*E*wan huffed and stepped forward. He pulled me into him, smoothed my hair in far too intimate a manner, and then planted a soft kiss atop my head.

"I'll see you tomorrow, Stell," he breathed and then extended me the length of his arms to give me a reassuring nod. He took his time letting go of my hands, lingering to run a thumb across my knuckles. I swear I heard a growl rumble through Gresham's chest. Ewan shot him a withering glance before leaving through the heavy doors.

Gresham consumed me then, his large body folding over mine. His presence was comforting, his embrace solid and safe. "I'd be happy to stay a while longer, Stella," he said. "I've known loss. Comfort is often found in company." He searched my gaze, his own guileless, concerned.

"No." I cleared my thick throat. "Thank you. I have Timbra. I'll be fine."

"All right," he agreed. "I'll find you tomorrow. Goodnight." I inclined my head and he traced away.

"You're exhausted, sweetie," Timbra said. "How about you put on your pajamas, I'll make some hot tea, and bring it to you in bed?"

That plan sounded wonderful.

"If you don't mind, I'll meet you upstairs in just a minute," I said. "I'd rather walk."

"Sure; whatever you need."

I dragged myself up the wide staircase, forcing one leg and then the next to take each step as a sort of cathartic punishment. By the time I reached the fourth floor I was so drained that I planned to fall flat on my face into my warm bed.

My plans for sleep were thwarted when I reached my room and Gresham stood just inside waiting for me.

"Uh. Hi," I said. "What's up? How did you get in here?"

"I traveled by intention. I've been here before. You obviously haven't warded against me." His smile was warm. Or maybe I just felt warm at the implication of having him in my room.

"Traced here," I corrected. "The kids call it tracing now."

"I'm not one of the kids."

"I've noticed."

"Have you?" His look held heat for the briefest moment, then he shook himself, seemingly remembering my present grief. He cleared his throat. "I came to make sure that you're all right. Being alone is when it's most difficult."

"Oh. Thank you. I'm so tired. I really planned to crash."
Didn't we just say goodbye not five minutes ago?

"Oh, well…" He ran a hand up the back of his neck and eyed the door.

"Stay for a bit, though," I said. "If you like." His posture eased at my invitation, and I offered the one chair in the room. I sat on the edge of my bed. Worst-case scenario, I'd just pass out and fall back into my pillow. Seemed a good plan.

We sat in contented silence for a while. Well, I was content. He was acting a bit agitated, like he had something to say.

He turned toward me in his chair and said, "Stella, I hate to be presumptuous, but now that your mother's gone and any insight on your father lost…well…you don't have anyone to teach you about your dragon. They're rare, mystical creatures. I happen to know something about them. I don't really have

177

anyone myself…" He searched for the right words. I had never before seen him flustered, but that's exactly what he was. "I am offering to be in your life," he blurted. "I'd like to be a part of your life."

Tears once again found their way out of my body. The stress of recent events, extreme mental exhaustion, and the affecting force of the friendship I'd experienced all combined to reduce me to a blubbering mess. Gresham rushed to my side and knelt beside the bed. He lay one hand on my knee and ran the other behind my head, smoothing my wild hair, wiping my tears.

I really wanted him to hold me again, to shelter me inside his big body. I scooted over and patted the warm bed. When he sat beside me I didn't think, I just threw a leg over and straddled him. I wrapped my arms around his big neck and tucked my head under his chin. Gresham sat stunned for a moment, but then circled my waist, returning my embrace and breathing deeply of my hair. I never looked back up, I just held on.

A

I woke slowly from the fog of sleep and despondency. The effects of crying myself to sleep had left me feeling hollow, sluggish.

My head, though full of cotton, began working before my body did and I realized with a horrifying start that I'd fallen asleep in Gresham's lap. I wondered how long he had let me sleep. I wondered if I'd drooled.

Yet embarrassed as I was, I was also warm and safe snuggled against him. In sleep I had nestled my nose to the side of his neck. I inhaled several times to savor the scent of him. He smelled, quite simply, like a man. His was a mix of masculine skin with undertones of cinnamon, leather, and a weighty earthiness. I'd never encountered such olfactory dynamite.

I was more than a little aroused.

The physical indication of his own arousal was pressing hard against me, intensifying the warmth between our bodies as I lay in his arms.

I raised my head to look in his eyes, and there I found a hunger that set my teeth on edge. But it wasn't fear that left my legs quivering. His gaze was intent, searching mine for a reading of my next move—would I be offended? Afraid? Would I run?

The thought of running did cross my mind. I knew if Gresham and I consummated this moment of lust things would change. For better or worse, I didn't know, but this was not a drunken mistake or an arrangement between 'buddies.' This was a calculated joining of two people who couldn't be more different, of people who had every reason to steer clear of each other. And probably should.

I dove at his mouth, sliding my tongue along his as I entered him. He met me with like force, his hot mouth covering mine. He was a skilled, passionate kisser. He played with my lips, playfully bit them, and ran his tongue along them for so long that I became lightheaded. He stroked an agile tongue against mine over and over so sensually that I lost conscious thought.

I could feel blood pumping furiously through my veins and….lower, which left me yearning for more attention. Gresham's kiss was carnal, demanding, and unbelievably lewd. In desperate need, I flexed against him for some small relief, but my body only screamed for more.

One of Gresham's hands clasped my ass and helped hold me to him. The other, at the back of my head, clutched my hair and pulled it down to expose my throat. He made his way down the side of my neck, the base of my throat, and the tops of my breasts, leisurely kissing the tops of them as he moved lower and lower.

I moaned so long and so loudly that I didn't hear the knock at my door. But Gresham had. He bolted up, eyes darting and head turned in order to concentrate on the sound. He looked so damned sexy coming up from my breasts that I was having trouble concentrating on anything else. I wanted him. Badly.

I inhaled to tell him so but realized it was Timbra who'd come to check on me. "I know you're home, Stell. You know these ears can pick up a cricket fifty yards away. Open up. I brought tea."

With a grunt that conveyed both frustration and resignation, Gresham stood. I righted my own clothes, then glanced up to see him looking back with obvious regret. His gaze shot away and I panicked. Did he regret the interruption, or what we had just so impulsively done?

For my part, I was left empty and aching. My body had anticipated so much more; had anticipated him, and the stark realization that I wasn't going to have him was crushing. I very seriously considered ignoring my friend outside, but the passionate moment was already lost.

"I'd better let her in before she finds a window," I said to break the tension.

"Yes," Gresham croaked, and then cleared the residual lust and disappointment from his throat. "She sounds determined. I should go, anyway." He ran a hand over his mouth and smoothed his hair, looking around to make sure he hadn't forgotten anything. He gave a slight shrug and lifted one corner of his mouth in a half-hearted smile. His face held confusion, but not cruelty, and I exhaled in relief as I supposed we hadn't ruined anything permanently. He turned and traced away.

I still wasn't used to the abrupt arrivals and departures that traveling by intention made possible. I didn't know if I ever would be.

I opened our adjoining bathroom door to let Timbra in, and she raked me from head to toe, trying to ferret out the circumstances. In the way that all women "just know," Timbra grasped the situation right away. Her big eyes swung to take in my tangled hair and mangled clothing.

"The hell was that?" she demanded and set the tea service on my buffet.

"*That* had the potential to be freaking fabulous, and you blew it," I replied, searching my cabinet for sugar.

"Ho, ho," she laughed, a wicked gleam in her eyes. "I guess we're even."

"Hmph." I guessed we were. She never had come clean about Boone. But I really wasn't in the mood to reveal all about Gresham, so I didn't press the matter.

"Gresham, huh?," she said. "I heard him in here."

"You heard, and still you interrupted?"

"Yes. I…I debated a while, but you'd had a lot to drink. And you're impressionable because of everything with your mom. I didn't want you to make a mistake."

"I'm a big girl, Timbra. I don't need a chaperone."

"I know that! I didn't know what the right thing to do was. I was concerned. I thought the best course of action was to prevent a mistake. You can always make it later."

I didn't answer, just eyed her irritably. She was right, of course. But I was a grown damned woman, and if I wanted to forget myself for a few moments after the shit couple of days I'd had, then I was certainly entitled to that.

"I hope you know I can't *help* but hear," she said defensively.

"Yeah, no wonder your adjoining suite was vacant."

She shot me a dirty look before eying me speculatively. "And Ewan?"

"What about Ewan?" I said. "He's adorable. I like him very much, though he *did* leave me to my own fate with a dragon. I certainly didn't plan for anything to happen with Gresham. Though I'd be lying if I said I haven't been attracted to him from the moment I saw him. It's a confusing time for me. Honestly, he was a welcome distraction."

"Ah. Well. Allow me to be the one to distract you now. The first order of business: showering. You look like you've been properly fucked."

"Too bad I haven't," I grumbled.

*O*nce more I stood at the front door of Gresham's stately manor after Pia had alerted me to an invitation for coffee. After the encounter in my room with Gresham, I'll admit to having taken a little extra time with my appearance than I probably would've otherwise. I threw on a black dress that was fitted at the waist and flared gently over my hips. I'd let my copper hair dry as it would, which today screamed "*Run those rough hands through me again.*"

My thoughts were all over the map about Gresham. Why had he invited me over? Did he regret what we did? I certainly didn't. And though I thought I maybe *should*, I did not feel like he'd taken advantage of me in a difficult time. If anything, I had needed both the distraction and the comfort. It felt *good* to feel good.

Gresham answered the door without revealing any emotion himself, and searched my face. "Hi," he said simply, his eyes crinkling at the corners when a genuine smile reached them.

"Hi," I repeated, unable to help neither the goofy grin nor the heat that spread across my cheeks.

Gresham led me to his kitchen, where the smell of coffee and something else decadent made my stomach rumble in appreciation.

"Is that French toast?"

He nodded wickedly. "You hungry?"

"Starving."

"Sit, sit. I'll bring it to you." I could sense his pleasure at my exuberance.

"And coffee?" I asked.

"And coffee." Again with the crinkly eyes. *Oh. So dreamy.*

Sealing his fate as a man I wanted very much to be naked with, Gresham brought steaming coffee, as well as real sugar and fresh cream. He made us both plates and sat across from me at the familiar banquette.

After a sip from his own cup, Gresham set it back down to the table before taking a deep breath. "So, last night was…"

"Wonderful." I said aloud at the same time Gresham finished with "unexpected."

"Dammit," I whispered and turned my head to the side. 'Unexpected' was not a good sign that he was thrilled with the turn of events.

"No, Stella, don't." He reached across the table to take my hand. "I don't mean that I didn't want it, too. It's just…I should never have let it go that far."

"That far?" I blinked with genuine confusion. Irritated crept in at the implication he should have stopped me sooner. "Just how far did you intend for it to go? I mean, you came to my room in the middle of the night. You knew I'd been drinking. And the fact you wanted me was evident not just in your eyes, Gresham." I darted my gaze pointedly at his pants.

"No, you're absolutely right. I should never have come to your room. It's not that I don't want you. I do. Too much. I have since you kicked me in the bollocks in your apartment…"

"I knew it. You perv."

"I… Dammit, Stella. I'm too old for you. I'm your mentor."

"Okay, Gresham, you've got what? Maybe 12 years on me? That's not the end of the worlds, m'kay?"

"Twelve? Twelve…" he trailed off in disbelief.

"Yes. Honestly, Gresham. You've gone on and on about
how everyone at Radix is an adult. I really don't get your
hangup with my age."

"Stella…I've been around for much longer than 30 years.
Sometimes I feel as if I have been around since the dawn of
time."

"What are you saying?"

"I was born *centuries* ago, not years. When you've teasingly
called me ancient, you've been more right than you knew."

"No," I said, certain that such things couldn't be possible.

"Yes. Stella, some species…some people of Thayer are—if
not immortal then very long-lived. You know this world is
steeped in the supernatural. Surely you can allow that a world
that facilitates traveling by intention is one that also supports
immortality."

"Tracing," I said numbly. "The kids call it tracing."

"Whatever the term, I have been doing it for a *very* long
time."

"No. It's not possible."

"Now you're just being obtuse."

"I'm not," I whined. "It's just a lot to take in. I need some
time to process." I thought for a moment. Then, "How long
are we talking here? I mean, are we talking Civil War old, or
ancient Roman civilizations old?"

He suddenly looked so tired. "I've seen ancient civilizations
rise and fall, Stella, and new ones rebuilt in their place. I've
known feasts and famine, crusades and renaissance. I've been
around long enough…long enough to know better."

Neither of us said anything for a long time. My mind reeled
with the new information, new concept. I really tried to accept
that Gresham was as old as Methuselah, but my mind only saw
him: his handsome face with the slightest crinkles at the
corners of his eyes. The strong body of a young man. What I
saw and what I heard were incongruent. I couldn't make them
meld. I decided to shelf the talk of ancient beings for the
moment and get back to the real issue at hand. 'When life gets

too real, focus on something else' was apparently my new motto.

"So, why did you invite me here, Gresham? Why be all sweet and flirty and make me breakfast?"

"I brought you here to talk as two adults and to resolve that despite our mutual attraction, I think it best we not become physical again."

"Not physical?" I asked.

"Yes."

"Platonic, then?"

"Exactly right."

"So, no steamy innuendo about 'throbbing chakras?' No references to the 'clitoris of the soul?'"

"Now just a minute. Those exercises were to help you find your form."

"Oh, please, Gresham. You talked to me like I was paying you by the minute. It took everything I had not to jump you right then and there. You know you were playing with me. You just admitted you've wanted me since we met. Don't give me that 'I'm your mentor' nonsense. I'd think you've been around long enough to grow a pair."

He narrowed his gaze as if he might argue, but didn't.

"I…I apologize. I did get caught up in the moment."

"You seem to do that a lot." I crossed my arms over my chest, letting out a breath I'd held too long.

"That's just it, I don't. At my age, I have certainly learned to control myself. And I've seen and done it all. Nothing has inspired me to lose my head in centuries. One more reason that we should end this now, before it goes any further."

Whatever that meant.

"Fine, Gresham. Platonic it is."

I was irritated. Not only because he was fooling himself— he had flirted with and shown interest in me since day one. But because ignoring the chemistry between us was both unnatural and unrealistic. But the rejection stung, too. I had gone to his home excited about the potential between us. He was *really* promising as a lover. And I liked him. Was he not into me? Was someone so *experienced* disappointed in my performance?

"I *am* sorry. I didn't mean to lead you on," Gresham concluded, all business.

Still steaming—and stinging—from his rebuff, I couldn't leave fast enough.

"Save it, Gresham. I've got to get back to The Root. Thanks for breakfast."

"I…ah…sure." He seemed uncomfortable, and rightly so.

I opened the front door to leave, but was met with a wall of fire. I screamed and jumped back as Gresham threw me behind him, sending me skidding across the foyer. A ear-splitting screech sounded just outside the large front windows before they, too, exploded in flames. Shards of glass scattered in my direction. I skittered away from the exterior walls as the house was attacked from all sides. The weighty turbulence of dragons' wings was unmistakable, and my knees buckled in response. Bone-deep, instinctual fear was my natural response to these fearsome creatures, and I knelt on the floor turning one hand over in the other.

"No, Gresham," I screamed from my position on the rug. He had seized a sword from a display in the sitting room. "Don't you have a gun?"

"Guns are useless against these things," he yelled over the deafening attack. "Bullets are impeded by scales."

"Skin is useless against fiery breath." I pointed hysterically to his sword-wielding arm.

"Why haven't my wards kept them at bay?" He cursed to himself as he ran to each window. "It's like there's no perimeter at all."

We watched in stunned silence as the largest of the three dragons dove straight for the house. We backed up together as it approached and ducked when the thing weightily crashed into the roof, causing chunks of plaster to fall from the ceiling.

"Goddammit!" Gresham rarely cursed. This was a bad sign. Very bad. "He's trying to tear a hole in the roof. My wards have obviously been breached. Stay here, Stella. Do you hear me? Stay here."

"Stay? But…" I fumbled for words. "Wh-where are you going?"

"I won't stand here to be slaughtered. They dare attack my home? I'll rip them apart."

A bark-colored dragon dove into the stonework and crumbled half of one chimney with its steely talons.

"With that sword? They're dragons, Gresham. Don't you have a storm shelter or a basement or something?"

There was no shame in my self-preservation game. All instincts pointed to 'flight' in this particular dilemma.

Gresham's eyes changed, then, and he looked as fearsome as the dragons. His irises were no longer amber, but a gleaming golden yellow that held movement like the burning sun. His pupils had stretched from their usual round to an eerie oblong. There was no longer a white to his eyes, just that burning, entrancing gold.

Gresham ran toward the front door in long, determined strides. I sat stunned as once he breached it, threw down the sword, and detonated into arrowed flight. My breath left me in a rush. I watched in awe as noble, grumpy Rowan Gresham was no more. In his place an obsidian dragon with eyes like the burning sun.

"Jeezuhs," I whispered. He was magnificent. And deadly.

Two of the three immediately attacked Gresham. Their agility despite their size staggered me. Big jaws snapped in fury while mighty tails lashed at him. Gresham wasn't on the defensive for long, though. As big, if not bigger, than the large red dragon, Gresham was a sight to behold. He flew straight up and out of the two's reach, then just as forcefully attacked them from above. He snatched the smaller dragon's scaly spine like an eagle clasping a fish, and swung it end over end across the sky.

"Yes," I yelped tin triumph, but ducked inside the house as the bark-colored attacker dove at me again. Racing to another window to watch the battle, I saw that Big Red had seized Gresham by a wing just after he released the smaller one.

"Gresham!" I screamed and ran out into the yard, fear for his life overriding my intellect.

He saw me, saw the impossible situation I'd put myself in as the brown dragon made a circling pattern overhead. Gresham launched the free half of his body toward Big Red's taloned grasp, rolling the punctured wing into itself and extending his long neck to gnaw at his attacker's gnarled claw. Big Red let go with an injured screech and Gresham dove toward me, for the smaller brown dragon circling me.

He threw the brown away with his claws, shoving it to the ground. The beast plowed through the fertile earth rolling shrubs and dirt into a mound like a small crater. All too soon it sat up in a daze, but then its face took on a vicious sneer when it realized the other two had Gresham on the run.

I was on my own.

That was all it took.

It's astounding what strength can be manifested when a girl finds herself out of options. I glanced briefly into the brown dragon's intelligent eyes. I shook my head with determination. I would *not* die today. I closed my eyes, inhaled deeply, and thought, "*Explode.*"

Free. I was free once again. And so powerful. I released my leathery wings with a whoosh and stretched my powerful neck.

I launched at the brown, roaring with malevolence. God, it felt so *good* to attack. So *right*. I knew I was born for it.

The brown backed away, scraping the sodded ground for purchase. The look in its eye wasn't fear, exactly, but recognition. It looked pointedly toward its cohorts in the sky, then, its mind seemingly made up, took off toward the east. After a final squawk to the others, the brown dragon faded into the morning sky, as intangible as evaporating dew.

Two left. I resolved to distract the smaller one from Gresham for a fair fight. I bolted into the air and dove at the small black one, intending to grasp the biggest target—its wings. It saw me approach, though, and extended powerful claws toward me, thinking to impale me before I reached it. I threw my big body wide and struck out with my heavy tail. I hit it in the stomach and a hiss of sparks flew from its hinged mouth.

The dragon's gaze swung to meet mine, not just furious but very obviously *mad*. One flick of intelligence cleared its wild eyes, though, followed by another. Its demeanor changed. I expected an attack, but without warning it, too, turned and fled, leaving only Gresham and Big Red in the violent throes of battle.

I started for the two, intending to help Gresham, but the brown approach again. I prepared for battle once more, excited to finish the fight. Eager for violence. Only the brown didn't approach me. It stopped just above Big Red, throwing its head back and screeching for attention. Big Red looked up, still fending off Gresham's skilled attacks, and it was as if the two communicated wordlessly.

Big Red glanced in my direction and disentangled itself from Gresham's grasp. Together the two remaining attackers vaulted straight up and out of sight, leaving me and Gresham confused. Wary.

After several moments with no sign of them again, I felt Gresham's stare.

"Let me in," he whispered faintly. It was his voice, but not exactly. It held more accent. That old-world European influence that I never could quite place. Shocked, I looked up at him. He blinked his big eyes in encouragement.

Let him in? How?

I'd had luck with my chakra, so I tried to relax that, but it wasn't right. I felt Gresham nudging at my brain and followed that clue. I found it. A gentle pressure inside my head. I worked to accept it and suddenly his speech was as clear as if he spoke to me. Clearer, really, since it was telepathically delivered.

"That was, without doubt, the most foolish thing I've seen you do. Stupid...Brave...Fierce. But foolish as hell."

"Next time I'll just let your ass fry, how about that?" I thought. Then, *"Gah! Did I just say that out loud? Not out loud. Did I think that and then you heard my thoughts?"*

"Yes, that's how telepathy works. I can hear your thoughts. Can we discuss the mechanics later? I fear they'll return. I have a plan."

"All righty. Shoot. This is awesome, by the way."

"Can you land and then change quickly back to human? We'll need to go directly to your room at Radix from the lawn. My wards are blown and we need to get to the protection of the school."

"Sure, I think so. Hey, Gresham. Did you see how badass I was back there? I was born to fight."

"Yes, yes. You're a regular Joan of Arc."

"You know, you really need some more current references. Calling me Joan of Arc dates you."

"Oh? Who do you suggest as a comparable current badass? Ripley?" he scoffed as much as possible within the confines of telepathy.

"Alien came out before I was born, Gresham. Good try, though. I really think of myself more a Daenerys Targaryen, considering the whole dragon angle."

"I'm unfamiliar with the name."

"Are you kidding me? You really are an old fart. And when I say old, I mean ancient. I bet you knew Joan of Arc."

"Sadly, she died at 19. I never met her." Crickets. He wasn't kidding.

"Stella. Why are we even talking about this right now? Land. Trace. Regroup."

"Gresham, you said trace. That's wonderful."

"I've always been a quick learner. Now land, dammit."

A

"When I agreed to this plan I didn't realize we'd both be standing here naked."

Gresham raised one shoulder. "Well. That's the thing about changing forms. A lot of enforced nudity. Best get used to it."

He stood before me without shame, his powerful presence taking up more space in the room than merely his body. Since the moment I saw him, I'd always found Rowan Gresham to be 'more.' I swallowed past the lump in my throat, my pulse suddenly racing.

Gresham's back was to me as he looked out my window for signs of trouble. I took the opportunity to appreciate his incomparable form. His powerful back was wide and chiseled with thick muscles. His wasn't the distended musculature of a body builder, but a more balanced manifestation of strength. As I raked down his body, definition at his shoulders caught my eye. Farther down the firm crease of his back a powerful ribcage slimmed into a tight waist. He had a good-sized scratch down his side, probably sustained during the fight. It looked to be healing well, though, and quickly. One firm crease disappeared, another taking its place. I shivered and stifled a groan of appreciation.

He turned around and held my gaze. "One thing you may not yet have noticed, Stella."

"Hmm?"

"Once you've found your form, some parts of you change forever. Senses, for example, remain heightened. Not to the level when in form, but stronger than they were before."

"Senses? You're saying I can see better? Hear better? I did know that, actually."

"Yes, and we can scent better, too," he said as he stalked toward me. "I smell your arousal now, for example."

I gasped. He was so bold, so comfortable with himself, with sexuality. I supposed that came from *centuries* of experience.

"That's not something said to someone you see platonically." God, I was in over my head with him.

"I've never seen you platonically. Who am I kidding?"

He was looking at my body. Hard. His gaze had wandered from my eyes and now hung heavily at my bare breasts. His breathing had become slower, more deliberate. He closed his eyes briefly, as if in gratitude, as he took in my nudity. His eyes became hooded, determined.

"You're trying to kid yourself if you think you can ignore the attraction between us," I said. *Look at me. I'm confident.* I was so not confident.

He didn't say another word. He strode toward me and stabbed a big hand into my loose hair. The other arm he snaked around my back to cup my naked hip and pull me toward him. Tucked so firmly into his hard body, my breasts were pressed into sexy round mounds. He looked down, darting his tongue along his full bottom lip.

My hips began to move against him. I could feel the heat of him against my belly as another kind of heat exploded through my core.

He attacked my mouth, his full lips encompassing my own. He sucked just under the edge of too hard, pulling my lips, nearly bruising them. As he held my face on both sides, his thumbs pressing together to purse my lips open, I had a fleeting thought of *too much*, but the pleasure was so great that I simply gave myself over to it. When he thrust his tongue into my open mouth with a growl I understood that this portion of the kiss was not intended for reciprocal participation. He scraped my lips with his teeth, letting go so suddenly that my abused little lips were bereft without his attention. Rowan Gresham was not kissing me, he was dominating me. And I was a-okay with that.

Sensual slowly replaced forceful, then sexy teasing replaced dominance. The kiss was an event all on its own. All I could do was hold on and enjoy the ride.

Yes. Perfect. Want. Mine. Faint fragments of thought ran across my mind, and I knew they weren't my own. As Gresham got lost in our impassioned frenzy, he'd lost his control. Encouragement and desire communicated during lovemaking had always turned me on. I loved it when guys talked to me— not demeaningly, but *dirty*. Gresham's uninhibited thoughts maddened me with desire.

He slowed, though, and the flattering thoughts I'd heard moments before were soon followed by some much less so. *Wrong. Stop. Truth.*

Gresham pulled back, gasping and looked away from me. He braced an arm on the doorframe, measuring his breaths to gain control.

"Gresham?" I asked. "Gresham, what's wrong? What 'truth?'"

Moments stretched without end as I waited for him to say something. Anything.

"I'm sorry," he croaked hoarsely before tracing out of sight.

I sat down abruptly on my bed, struggling to gain my own composure and wondering what the hell had just happened. What. A. Day.

"Stella, a physical communication has been accepted for you at Sabre Hall's front desk," Pia intoned somberly.

I was getting used to waking to her voice.

"Physical communication...?"

"A letter," she supplied.

"Who's the letter from, Pia?"

"A messenger delivered the communication. There is no return information. You may retrieve it from the front desk."

"Telepathy, talking PDAs...all this magic and technology and still I must physically descend stairs and retrieve a hand-written letter."

"You can always trace," Timbra hollered helpfully from her room across the bath. Those ears. She was right, though. I really needed to learn to think like a Thayerian if I was going to make this my home.

Once back in my room I opened the sealed envelope. The letter inside was written with a flourishing script, and I had some difficulty making it out.

I bet Gresham's old ass could read this, I thought sarcastically, then realized with no sarcasm at all that he was actually was perfect for the job.

I had Pia send a copy to him, and waited. In a matter of moments he knocked on my door. His face was ashen and he stepped stiffly inside.

"What is it, Gresham? What's wrong?"

"This letter is from Brandubh's dragons—the ones that attacked us yesterday… They say they're your mother's people."

A

"Gresham, before we do this, don't you think an explanation about yourself and your past is way overdue? And what the hell happened last night? You took off like the devil himself was after you."

"I…what do you mean?"

"Oh, stop stalling. You know exactly what I mean. You've been alive for 'centuries,' but won't specify how long. You transformed into a dragon, yet had never let on we had that in common. You've revealed next to nothing about yourself, yet you know me…intimately. It's not fair, and I want some answers."

At my reminder, his eyes closed briefly before darting to my bed and then back to me. I feared my inquisition was in danger of being derailed, so I pressed on before he could act on any of the ideas that were so obviously forming in his head.

"If my mother was thought to be the last existing dragon, yet we have just learned that was not true, how do *you* fit into all of this? Surely you aren't some ancient forebearer of mine?" *Ew.*

"No, no. Nothing like that; don't be ridiculous."

"Well, I'm grasping at straws here because I have nothing to go on. You said you wanted to be in my life, Gresham. How can we move forward if you can't trust me?"

"I trust you." He ran his hands through the hair at his temples, pulling back so far that the skin around his eyes tightened. "I choose to keep some things close to my chest for now. When the time is right, I'll tell you everything." His rigid posture indicated that the subject was closed.

Maybe the day before I would have accepted his answer, but I was sick and tired of learning tidbits of information here and there when he decided to dole them out. I was also a little hurt that after what we'd shared he still refused to trust me, to open up. I was the only one left exposed.

"I bet *Livia* knows," I sneered. Not my best moment.

"Livia does know a lot. She and I were lovers for a very long time."

Ouch.

"How long?"

"Long enough."

"Dammit." I was getting nowhere. *'Long enough.'* Asshole. "Wait a minute," I said, stunned. "You're not saying that she's...immortal, too?"

"Immortal? No. Enough, Stella. Do you want to arrange a meeting with the dragons or not?"

He had a good poker face, but I was catching on to his tactics. He wouldn't lie, but he would sure evade and mislead before changing the subject. I knew I'd get no further with him, though, and let the subject lie. I did want to meet my mother's people, if that was who they truly were.

A

"This meeting is going to be tricky. And dangerous," Gresham warned.

"Yes, I agree. If they want to meet me while Brandubh's away, it's only logical there's a chance he'll return."

"My biggest fear is that this whole thing is a trap."

Gresham paced my room. His apprehension was almost palpable.

"It's possible," I admitted. "But I have to go. I have to know."

"Mmmph," was his only reaction.

"You don't have to go, Gresham, really. This entire thing is about me. My mother. My relatives. My future. I can trace there and quickly back if I get into trouble."

Gresham jerked. "I'll not let you go alone. Don't be ridiculous." I had insulted his masculine pride. He had a lot of that.

"I've been looking for information on these dragons for centuries," he said fiercely. "And if you think I'll miss an opportunity to learn more about Brandubh, then you're woefully deceived."

"Wait a minute, Gresham. They've invited me there under a white flag. You can't hurt them."

"I'll make no promises, Stella."

"But they're possibly my relatives. They're my only source of information. I need them."

"They attacked my home yesterday; they tried to kill us."

"No, they backed off once they recognized me. You know they did. No one was hurt yesterday. No harm was done, Gresham."

"They did a hell of a lot of harm to Caraway," he bellowed.

"Well, I am sorry about the damage to your home. But if you won't promise not to hurt them, then I won't allow you to come, Gresham. I'm serious about that."

He took two steps toward me, which put him far too close. He breathed two or three heavy breaths before visibly calming down. "I'm going. We're going. At the first sign of trouble, promise me you'll trace back to The Root."

"All right. I'm not stupid, Gresham. At the first sign of anything weird, I'll trace back."

He nodded, and though the situation was tense, we had an agreement.

"There's nothing at the location they gave but an old volcanic crater. It's barren and dangerous. No one has any reason to go there…which makes it a perfect hideout for three massive dragons," he trailed off. "It must be warded. Surely someone would have stumbled upon them before now."

"Or if they did, the dragons made a quick flambé." I cringed the moment it escaped my lips.

My mouth had opened before my brain kicked in. Again. Though the thought did bring up difficult subject matter. If these dragon people were in fact my relatives, how did I feel about that? About them? People died the night of the attack on Caliph Square. They tried to kill *me*. Were they responsible for the Steward Massacre, along with my mother? Were these people monsters, as well as dragons? What the hell was I walking into?

I seriously considered suggesting to Gresham that we abandon the meeting and use the location they revealed to destroy them, ridding my new homeland of a long-known enemy and threat. But that course of action would steal from me the only real lead I had on knowledge of my family, of my mother...of myself. No, I would ride this thing out. I wanted information, and the opportunity to find it had fallen into my hands. If we had to go to war with them after this, so be it.

Having been to the base of the crater before, Gresham traced us there. It was taller than I'd imagined; we were at the base of a mountain twenty miles north of the city. No vegetation or trees grew around it, or along its sides. Deep gray and charred, the crater was ominous and just plain creepy. I was compelled to leave the moment we stepped foot atop the blackened dust.

"What now? Are we to climb it?" I asked.

"I'm not sure."

I was stumped at how to proceed. That Gresham was, too, wasn't encouraging.

I walked the perimeter of the structure in search of a mystical trap door, or a hidden lift…anything.

I was so shocked when I found the entrance that I said nothing for several moments, which Gresham noticed right away.

I used to love to look at those 3D pictures designed to fool the eyes. Upon first glance they were a pattern, nothing more. But then if I stared long enough and let my eyes cross a little another image appeared. The entrance was like that. I would have missed it; Gresham *did* miss it. But I noticed the faintest indication of something more—just a slight wobbly spot in the air surrounding the entrance. And when I looked, really looked hard, the three-dimensional aspect of a crevice hidden by an outcropping of rock revealed itself. Once I saw it, I couldn't not see it, and wondered how I'd ever missed it. Just like those puzzles I remembered.

"Shall we?"

Gresham nodded solemnly, and we walked side-by-side into the dark opening.

A cold, dank corridor had been chiseled through the body of the mountainous crater long ago. It was just tall enough that Gresham didn't have to bend his big frame. Fire-lit torches lined the corridor, though not frequently enough to shed any light on the space. The flickering beacons only served to indicate the direction of the path. We walked silently in the darkness together. I admit to grabbing the waistband of Gresham's pants on one or two occasions as creepy little things that loved the dark skittered across my feet. Beyond one last torch, we spotted daylight through the end of the corridor. I let out a breath, and Gresham squeezed my hand in reassurance.

We stood on either side of the mouth of the corridor, unsure what to do next. What if it was a trap? What if the moment we stepped from the protection of the cave and into the light we became walking torches? I vacillated between leaving before we caught their notice and storming in as my dragon.

The decision was made for us when a deep voice slid across my brain.

"*Come in. We know you are there,*" it said. Since I'd had telepathic experiences with Gresham, brain muscle memory kicked in, and I 'heard' the wordless communication right away.

"*Who have you brought, little dragon?*" the voice asked. "*Is he the one who fought for you?*"

"*Yes,*" I said. "*He's my friend. Who are you?*"

"*Rowan Gresham is no friend to dragons,*" the voice boomed inside my head.

"*What do you mean? He is a dragon.*"

"Let's go in," said Gresham.

"I'm coming in with Gresham. If you try to hurt us, you'll be sorry." Bluster, bluster, bluster.

We stepped into the light then, both covering our eyes at the sudden brightness. When I could see again, I found the three dragons that had attacked Gresham's house.

They sat upright, fearsome heads held high. Big Red was much larger than I remembered now that I was so close to him and in human form. Scales the size of my hands shone in the sun, his a Chinese red to my auburn. If we were, in fact, related, this was almost certainly a family trait since my mother, too, was a redhead. I had a sad little moment and wondered if her coloring as a dragon was copper and auburn, like mine, or Big Red's brighter scarlet.

"Aye, your dragon resembles Edina's."

"Oh. I hadn't realized I said that out loud…err…thought it. You know what I mean."

"What of your mother, then? Is she dead?"

"She disappeared. Very recently."

"I'm sorry," Big Red chuffed at the same time the smaller brown said, *"Oh. Dear Edina."*

I nodded.

"I'm Eiven," Big Red said. *"Brother of your mother. This is my son, Stryde, and of course you've met Bay, my mother."*

"Your mother? Then…I have a grandmother?" A seedling of hope dared sprout through the cracked soil of my broken heart.

Never mind that she was the one who tried to impale me the night of Solstice Fest. And dive-bombed me at Gresham's house. Bygones.

"Aye, love. I'm your granny. Stryde's your cousin and Eiven your uncle."

"Relatives? Then…wh…why were you trying to kill me?" I sounded far more pitiful than I intended, my voice coming out in a high-pitched whine.

Big Red—Eiven—jumped in quickly. *"We didn't know you were our kin. We were…ordered to retrieve a girl called Stella Stonewall.*

It had been so long since we were let out of this prison that we jumped at the chance. But Bay saw that you were one of our own, and you looked so much like Edina…"

"We couldn't have known the name, you see? We were just looking for a girl," explained Bay. "Edina disappeared so long ago. Changed her name, I suppose. She was a Drakontos. We all are."

"Drakontos," I repeated the unfamiliar family name. My name, if they were to be believed. "Are there more of you? Of us?"

"Afraid we three…well, four now…are the last of the Drakontos. The last of any of the dragon lines," said Eiven.

"No, there's Gresham, too," I reminded. "He's like us."

"Mr. Gresham is nothing like us, Stella."

"What do you mean? You saw his dragon yourself."

"You said you were ordered to retrieve Stella," Gresham cut in. "Was it Brandubh who gave the command?"

Eiven gave a slow nod.

"Are you his prisoners, then? Unwilling henchmen, like my mother?"

"We are," said Bay before closing her deep-set eyes. "We have been for a very long time." She stretched her leathery neck, and for the first time I noticed that she was wearing some sort of torque—they all were.

"If you're compelled to do his bidding, how were you able to flee when you recognized Stella?" Gresham asked.

"We felt strongly enough that we were able to resist. But there was a price. There's always a price for disobedience."

Eiven turned and made a movement with his shoulder—one that would have flexed his mighty wing had it not been clipped to the quick. All three dragons' wings had been savagely cleaved.

I stifled a gasp with a shaky hand to my mouth.

"They'll grow back. Eventually."

The one Eiven had indicated as Stryde paced back and forth, jerking his butchered wing sockets repeatedly. He mumbled something over and over and seemed on the verge of hysterics.

They all looked shamed and miserable. That they made this sacrifice for my benefit wasn't lost on me, but I didn't know what to say. The protracted silence became uncomfortable.

"*When was the last time you saw my mother?*" I blurted. I still had so many questions.

"*Not for a very long time,*" sighed Eiven. "*She once lived here, with us. When Thayer retaliated for the Gnome and Fae, we fought brutally for many years. They killed our kind one after another, and we feared for our lives. We were so tired of fighting, of death. Edina was favored by Brandubh, and she used that advantage to try and help us all escape. He discovered her plan, though, and isolated her as punishment. That is where she eventually met your father.*"

"*Did you see her again after that? Did you know my father?*"

"*Aye, we saw her again. Once she and your father escaped, they attempted to set us free. They came here in an effort to remove our torques, but Brandubh caught them. He always knows. They waged a mighty battle. Brandubh thought Edina too meek, too afraid of him to do any real harm. But once free of his constraints she backed him into a corner and readied to tear his evil head from his body. Brandubh was so furious that she dared betray him he reached around her and struck out against your father in retribution. He hit him with some sort of debilitating spell in the shoulder—any closer to his chest and he would have died where he stood. Though wounded, your father was able to take form, and swung his tail to knock Brandubh into the mountainside.*"

"*Wait. Swung his tail? My father was a wolf. He couldn't have done much damage with a tail.*"

"*Your father was a wolf, 'tis true,*" said Bay. "*He was also a dragon, a falcon…he could change into anything he'd ever seen. Your father was no' just a wolf, Stella. He was an omni.*"

"*A wha?*"

"*That's nonsense,*" Gresham said. "*There are very few lines of omnies left, and I know them all.*"

"*I don't care a whit who you know,*" Bay bit out. "*Gabrio Shaw was an omni.*"

"Gabrio Shaw," I whispered, forgetting telepathy in my astonishment. "I never knew his name."

"*What are…er…omnies?*" I asked, first looking at the dragons and then to Gresham, who'd gone still as death. All of the color drained from his face, making him look dead, too.

"*Later, Stella,*" Gresham choked.

"*I am sick of your high-handedness, Gresham.*"

"*Not. Now.*" Gresham ground the words out between clenched teeth.

"*Yes, now. I won't be put off or ignored any longer.*"

Gresham turned from me, completely putting me off and ignoring me.

"*I assume you summoned Stella for a reason,*" Gresham addressed the three. "*And if you've been trapped here alone for so long, how were you able to contact her at all? How did you send a messenger to Radix?*"

"*I'll take that question.*" A new voice slithered through my brain—one laced with both cruelty and confidence. "*I sent the messenger.*"

"*I'm sorry, love,*" whimpered Bay, backing into the side of the crater as her pitiful stumps shuddered nervously. "*He…he forced us.*"

"*Trace, Stella,*" Gresham said. "*Don't hesitate, just go.*" When I didn't move he reached for my arm, but I jerked away. "*Go,*" he demanded, his face tight with anger; with fear.

"Are you kidding me?" My voice rose in anger. "You three stood there chatting us up this whole time knowing this was a trap? What the hell is wrong with you people? Haven't you seen enough death and suffering?"

"*Indeed we have.*" Stryde seethed. Though this was the first real time that he'd communicated since our arrival, his anger came through the lines of telepathy loud and clear. His maddened pacing stopped as he addressed me.

"*We have seen more death and torture and suffering than one such as you can imagine. For hundreds of years we've suffered not just from our imprisonment, but from our own regret. From self loathing. We've been trapped here, slowly losing our grips on reality. Can you imagine what it is like not just to watch your only family—the only ones left of your kind— slowly go mad, but to know that your own mind is growing weak? And to*" *be powerless to do anything about it? No, you cannot imagine, I assure you. Brandubh offered me freedom in exchange for your capture, and I took it. I took it gladly. "*

"That's enough, son," barked Eiven. *"She's not our enemy. She's just a pawn in his game as we all are."*

"Pawns, knights, queens," intoned the as-yet-unseen owner of the voice. *"Yes, you all have a part to play in my game."*

Stryde's gaze shot wildly back and forth. He was terrified of Brandubh. It was beyond odd to see a grown dragon tremble with fear at the sound of a man's voice.

I swallowed involuntarily, my mouth gone dry with fear. The sorcerer was obviously powerful enough to imprison and abuse not just my mother, but three creatures whose fearsomeness was unparalleled. Would Eiven, Bay, and Stryde stop us if we tried to flee? I had yet to lay eyes on Brandubh, but I thought it was probably time to jet. Gresham was beyond ready. Was Brandubh just toying with us—playing cat and mouse, making us believe we had a chance to escape only to knock us back into the rocky side of the cratered mountain? I looked to Gresham, wondering what our next move should be.

To the untrained eye, Gresham appeared cool and collected, but I could see the tightening clenches of his jaw. He caught my gaze and gave an almost imperceptible nod.

I lifted my foot to trace home…and nothing happened. I tried again with the same result.

"I can't trace, Gresham," I whispered urgently.

"Neither can I. Must be some sort of ward against it."

"What now? What now?" I was whining and may have been approaching hysterical.

"Now, we fight."

"No. *Let's run. We can make the cave, leave through the corridor the way we came."*

"It's too late for that. You know as well as I that either Brandubh or one of your charming relatives will have us before we can escape. They've planned on it. On my word, run toward the cave. I'll distract them. Run as far and fast as you can. You can likely trace once on the other side of the corridor."

205

"*Oh, like I'm just going to abandon you here to fight three dragons and an infamous evil sorcerer.*"

"*I've won a lot of unfair fights in my time, Stella. I'm still here, aren't I?*"

"*Yeah, but...*"

Any further argument was cut off when Brandubh himself materialized in front of us.

The mighty dragons stood at our backs, pitting us between them and Brandubh. The ominous display had its intended effect—I was scared as hell.

Brandubh's appearance and what I had expected 'the evil sorcerer' to look like were two very different things. Very different. He wasn't weathered and bitter. He didn't have a ferret-like face or a pot belly. There wasn't a white beard in sight, and the wind didn't mystically whip around his wizard's robe.

But he was tall. Impossibly wide. And well-dressed in sensible dark linen slacks and a charcoal tunic. Methodical, clear blue eyes pierced mine from beneath a heavy brow. He hadn't shaved, but I suspected that was more a result of planning an image than a lack of effort. Brandubh was particular in his appearance. Meticulously so. His dark hair was closely shorn and silvered along the temples.

He smiled like a fox biting a hen's tail through a wire coop.

"Ah, Stella," his voice slithered through my head though he spoke aloud. "How I've dreamed of this day. You're as lovely as your mother. I wonder, are you as sweet?"

Weird thing to say. I glanced at the dragons, who shuffled uncomfortably when I searched their eyes for answers. *Oh, ew.*

"What do you want, Brandubh?" Gresham growled.

"Mr. Gresham. As rigid and unprepared as ever."

"Wait, you've met him before?" *More mothereffin' secrets.*

"Not. Now."

"What? Your 'friend' did not reveal our association to you, Stella?" Brandubh asked.

"We have no association, you psychotic asshole, just a history. One I plan to dissolve today."

"As if you could. You'll never win. Have you not learned this by now?" Brandubh laughed, his steely eyes glittering with genuine mirth.

"But back to your question, Mr. Gresham. You might as well know now. I'm going to find great pleasure in taking her from you."

Gresham growled low in his chest and snarled viciously. His fierce reaction scared *me*, and I was the least likely recipient of his wrath.

Brandubh continued as if Gresham hadn't made a sound. "I know you've had her; I can smell you all over her. Doesn't matter. I have plans for this little red one."

He eyed me appraisingly, as if I was a prime heifer paraded into a sale lot.

"Due to the loss of most of my dragons by your petulant people, I've had no way to replenish my herd. I'd thought to use this one to breed, but she's too old and isn't fecund." He nodded in the direction of Bay.

"Everything changed when I saw this little *vibria* enter Thayer." Brandubh laughed almost giddily. "I have two prime drakes with which to breed her. She can make her choice or they can fight for her; I care not."

"You sick sonofabitch. That's my uncle; my cousin." My stomach, already tight with fear, roiled in disgusted.

Brandubh circled me, appraising me with a calculating eye that made my skin crawl. I turned as he circled, never giving him my back completely.

"In this line of business, close bloodlines are a triviality." He stopped circling. "Gresham, she positively reeks. Did you roll in her? Not that it will deter me. Your claim on her is as weak as the wards on your home."

Gresham went rigid at the mention of the attack on Caraway Manor.

"Oh, don't look so shocked. Your arrogance will always be your downfall. Did you really think you could protect against me, against my dragons, forever? Once I removed the source of your wards' power they wilted like sauteed greens."

Gresham squeezed his eyes shut in pain or regret; I couldn't tell which. I wondered what source Brandubh referred to.

"Now, where was I? Oh, yes. Inbreeding. Actually, when used properly, inbreeding can be an effective husbandry program. Inbreeding superior specimens creates exceptional offspring."

"How can this possibly make sense to you? I would never agree to that."

"Oh, I can force you...or they can. The young black one is particularly keen on the idea, though I think it's less about you, and more about doing violence." He stopped circling again and whispered conspiratorially, "He's quite mad, you may have noticed."

"*Run, Stella.*" Gresham's deep voice roared through my brain.

For once in my life I didn't argue with him. The whole lot of the group was freaking nuts, and even I knew it was impossible to win a fight against crazy.

I sprinted toward the cave entrance, my arms pumping furiously as my legs propelled me toward the safety of the corridor. I was almost there when a blast of rock and dust blinded me. I skidded to a halt, and when the dust cleared I saw an avalanche of stony debris had blocked the corridor.

Wild with uncertainty, I turned around to find Gresham, who was grappling with Brandubh. The two traded vicious punches and holds, but neither could keep the other in grasp. Brandubh was powerful, but Gresham was savage. I stood, stunned, and watched as he bloodied the powerful sorcerer with his hands.

Brandubh shook himself, seeming to remember that his own power was not limited to the physical. He chanted slowly, deliberately at first, but Gresham popped him in the mouth. Then the words poured furiously from his lips. His body seemed to grow, but it was less his physical form than his...aura. He had just called a powerful magic into himself.

Brandubh smiled, his eyes widening with anticipation and insanity. He backhanded Gresham across the face, sending him flying through the pitted interior of the crater. He hit the side of the mountain, the crack of bones audible across the pit, and slid roughly down the face of the rock. He never stopped his fall. I waited, but Gresham didn't rise. He lay face-down in the rubble. Dead or debilitated, I didn't know.

I looked to the dragons, their betrayal chewing at my heart like rats at a round of cheese. Eiven and Bay sat stock still, avoiding Brandubh's notice and presumed wrath. Stryde's big body racked with tremors—I suspected from the exertion of resisting his barely-leashed violence.

Brandubh's sights were on me, and he stalked toward me.

I was relieved when I sensed the familiar stirring of my chakra. I lovingly embraced the change and my dragon rippled out. I stretched to my full height, my copper scales and reddened wings chuffing as I prepared to fight. I watched Brandubh closely, my reptilian eyes trained on his every move.

"There she is," rasped Brandubh. "My auburn beauty."

He held something shiny and it glinted when it caught the sun. I squinted to see that he was concealing a torque—one obviously intended for me. I would not suffer the same fate as my mother, as the three Drakontos dragons. Enraged, I bellowed from deep in my soul and released a current of fire that would have decimated a bunker.

Brandubh shook his head in mock admonishment. "Fireproof," he pointed up and down his body. "And, master of dragons," he said with a snarl.

With one flick of his wrist, he pulled my dragon from me and left me wheezing and naked on the ashen ground.

"What do you think, huh, boys?" he said obnoxiously. "Not bad. Not bad…though you've been in your dragon forms so long you probably prefer her the other way. Am I right? Ah, well. Plenty of time for both."

Something flicked in my periphery. I recognized the premonition right away and squinted to see the vision. The scratchy scene that played out revealed Brandubh bending and lifting me by the back of my hair. I cried out in pain, and he only shook me harder, like a puppy held by the scruff.

A puppy. An idea struck.

Mere seconds later Brandubh bent to lift me by the hair. A slow smile spread across my face and I looked the maddened sorcerer dead in the eye.

"What's so funny, little dragon?" he sneered.

"I know something you don't know."

"Oh? What's that?"

"Not just dragon," I croaked. "Omni, like my father."

I burst into my wolf form, sparing no time to snarl or slaver. I dove for his throat and tore at the spongy esophagus and brittle spine behind it. I shook my head, growling, sending blood and other bits flying into the dirt.

Brandubh threw me from him with a magical jolt, and I landed roughly at Eiven's feet.

The sorcerer struggled to rise up on his arms and spared one look at me that betrayed both his bewilderment and fury before he disappeared as abruptly as he'd arrived.

I spat out pieces of Brandubh's fleshy throat and ejected my tongue repeatedly, like a dog in peanut butter, trying to rid myself of his vulgar taste.

I ran to Gresham's side, sliding onto human knees as I reached him.

I rolled him onto his back. Felt for a pulse. It was there. Faint as a whisper, but it was there. I lifted his head onto my lap and shook him. His body was limp, his breathing shallow.

I shook him again. Nothing. I ran my hands obsessively over his face and head, unsure of what to do next.

I patted his face and beat his chest, my efforts turning progressively more rough. I panicked and my chest thumped and burned, but there was nothing my beasts could do now.

"Gresham," I sobbed as I leaned over his body. "Wake up. Please," I pleaded with his unconscious form.

Moments dragged on for hours as I monitored his breathing, unable to do anything but hope that he would come to.

He groaned at first, but as consciousness set in he immediately stiffened and tried to rise.

"Brandubh," he rasped.

"Gone," I said weightily, and helped him sit up.

"How?"

"I changed into my wolf and bit his motherfucking throat out, that's how. I *told* you I was a badass."

"You? Killed Brandubh?"

"Oh, I don't think he's dead. We're not that lucky. He's in pretty rough shape, though, and I doubt he'll be back here today."

Gresham nodded and searched the cavernous terrain. He stood. Wobbled a bit, but caught himself.

"You know, Gresham, you always underestimate me. I really think it's time I had a title—something indicative of my savagery."

Satisfied that Brandubh was indeed gone, he turned to me and quirked a brow. "Like a nickname?"

"Yeah, a nickname. Something like Stone-cold Stonewall? Stella the Sorcerer Slayer? Dragon Lady is too genteel. Oh! I know—Hell Bitch, like Call's horse. That's intimidating."

"Call? What are you talking about?"

"It's a Lonesome Dove reference. I thought sure you'd know that one. Grumpy old farts love Lonesome Dove."

"For the hundredth time, I am not a grumpy old... Stella. Did you know you're naked?"

"Hmm?" I looked down at myself and waved away any concern. "Oh. Well, that's the thing about changing forms. Lots of forced nudity. Best get used to it."

"Oh, I can definitely get used to it," Gresham said wickedly, and pulled me into him.

Thank You for Reading

Dear Reader,

I hope you enjoyed *Rare Form* (*Descended of Dragons, Book One*). Things are getting good with Stella and Gresham, aren't they? Readers have written asking, "What's next for Ewan?" or "Will Boone and Timbra make it?" If you really want to know, check out *Origin Exposed*, Book Two in the series, which was selected by iTunes/iBooks as "Our Pick" in Fantasy/Sci-Fi.

I realize you have a lot of options when choosing a book, and I want to thank you for choosing to read this one. I love hearing from readers, and I love feedback. Tell me what you liked, what you loved…even what you didn't love. You can write me at authorjencrane@gmail.com or visit my site at www.JenCraneBooks.com

Lastly, please consider leaving a review of Rare Form wherever you buy books. Reviews help other readers find books they might love, and they help authors in many ways, too.

Thanks so much for reading, and thanks for supporting me and my books.

Jen

Enjoy this preview of

DESCENDED OF DRAGONS
BOOK 2

BY
JEN CRANE

*Origin Exposed was selected by iTunes/iBooks
as "Our Pick" in Fantasy/Sci-Fi.*

I sat wrapped in Rowan Gresham's strong arms thankful for my life and his.

His warm skin was a welcome contrast to my own as I pressed my cheek to his chest and absently nuzzled his wide shoulder.

My efforts to relax, to relish the comfort and security Gresham's presence lent were useless. My bare legs trembled to the beat of an erratic heart. What started as a light tremor grew stronger until the physical manifestation of my shock intensified to a full-blown shake. I snapped my knees together and wrapped my arms around them. If the traitorous things insisted on vibrating, I would constrict them into serenity.

My plan didn't work.

I was a ragged mess from the aftermath of the fight with Brandubh, and bewildered to learn not only did I *have* living relatives, I was descended of dragons who were feared, hated.

I was a ragged mess from the aftermath of the fight with Brandubh, and bewildered to learn not only did I have living relatives, but I was descended of dragons who were feared, hated.

And my father—about whom I'd sought information my entire life—was a magical breed I'd never heard of: an *omni*. It was urgent that I learn more about him, as well as the dragons. It just so happened I had a captive audience of three such dragons.

But as I scoured the mountainous crater in which they'd been imprisoned for centuries, I found no one. My stomach seized at the realization Gresham and I were the only two left on the rocky battlefield. The Drakontos dragons had traced away as we celebrated our victory over the powerful sorcerer Brandubh.

"Gresham."

"Hmm?" He'd recovered quickly and was absently nuzzling my neck. His breath was hot on my collarbone and his hand crept dangerously close to my naked ass.

"Gresham," I said. "The dragons are gone."

His dark head snapped up, amber eyes wild as they bounced around the crater. He jerked his hand from me in confused horror. *Like I'd put it there.*

"Dammit," Gresham growled and stood to his full height. "Dammit!" His curse reverberated through the cratered mountain's interior, echoing his frustration. His hands formed tight fists at his sides. "I can't believe I let them get away," he said and began to pace. His every move was rigid with anger. "He'll have my job for this. My job, hell," he spat, "he'll have my head. And rightly so. I had four of Thayer's prime enemies in one place and let them escape. Right under my damn nose."

"Well, that's not really fair, Gresham," I said. "You were knocked unconscious. Brandubh nearly killed us both. He may have gotten away, but just barely. And he must be badly injured if the dragons were able to trace away and escape him."

"He'll heal. They'll heal," he said, kicking a pile of rocks that sent stone and dust flying in a wide arc. "I had them all here and could do nothing. I couldn't use my magic, couldn't trace. It was stupid to come here alone with you. I underestimated him and inflated my own ability. Dammit!" He stopped pacing and looked me up and down, a scowl replacing his handsome features. A snarl gathered his lips into a bitter pinch. "I continue to make poor decisions where you're concerned, behaving like a teen-aged boy trying to impress a girl."

On some level I preened with pleasure to hear the enigmatic man admit he lost his senses around me, that he wanted to impress me. I'd longed to wow him since the moment I first saw him. But I was also wary of the admission. Rowan Gresham was sharp, and not just intellectually. I feared if he suspected his feelings for me compromised him he'd have no reservations about cutting me off.

Gresham continued to curse himself, stomping aimlessly within the crater and mumbling as he stabbed his hands through the hair at the sides of his head.

I tried to deflect some of his stress by pointing out the things we had accomplished. "We may not have captured Brandubh," I said, "but we learned a lot that could help the authorities. Not only is he still very much alive, but his interest in ruling—or destroying—Thayer still exists."

Gresham's eyes compressed to a tight squint. "You're saying that like it's a good thing."

"No...I mean... We learned about his sick dragon-breeding plan. We stopped it. And because we injured him so badly, his remaining dragons were able to escape. He has nothing now."

"Oh, Brandubh will always find a way. Dragons or no, he'll never stop." Gresham stopped his pacing to face me. "I know you're trying to find the positive in the situation, Stella. But let me tell you how the leader of Thayer, the people of Thayer, will see it. I was the first one to see Brandubh in centuries. I stood within feet of him, fought him. Not only did I *not* capture him, but a little girl fought him for me. I allowed him to escape. *And* I failed to discover where he's been hiding all these years."

"I think you're taking this far too personally," I said, but he ignored me. His rant amped even louder, his voice booming throughout the cavernous space.

"I discovered that three of the dragons responsible for the Steward Massacre—until now thought eradicated—are alive. I didn't capture them. No, I allowed them to escape, too, and have no idea where to begin looking for them. Worse, the dragons know I know they exist. They'll assume we're coming for them and go into hiding. Or come for us first."

I crept toward him and reached to console him, but he jerked away before I could touch him. "Why are you acting like it's your sole responsibility to save Thayer," I asked. "I mean, sure, we're taught at Radix we're supposed to defend our home, but it wasn't your job alone, Gresham. You fought Brandubh; you nearly had him. I injured him, and we cost him his most valuable weapons. Not a bad day."

"Stella," Gresham said, his face crumbling into a tortured mask, "it *is* my job. I've been protecting the people of Thayer since long before you were born."

"But..." I paused, trying to comprehend. "What do you mean? What're you saying?"

Gresham slammed his eyelids shut. He clenched his teeth with such force I saw the muscles working in his square jaw.

"Gresham? You said you did 'special projects.' I knew you were being intentionally vague, but...what...what are you saying?"

He let out a ragged breath and found my gaze. His eyes were pained. Shamed. "There is much I didn't—couldn't—tell you at first. I should've told you when you first found your wolf, but by then I felt such guilt. And I was shocked to find that I *gave a damn*, Stella. I didn't want to see the disappointment in your eyes. I knew you'd find out eventually. I'm surprised it took this long. It only did because you're an outsider and your friends are all primos. I thought for certain the Redfern girl would recognize me from my dealings with her father, or one of those boys you associate with would piece it together."

Blood rushed to my face, my ears. I heard white noise, a faint but consistent background to our conversation.

"What the hell are you talking about, Gresham?" My voice rose as I grabbed at his arm and pulled him around to face me. "Tell me what?" My face was fevered and I felt the familiar sting of tears threatening to form.

"Stella," he said reverently, smoothing the auburn hair back from my face. He bent to run his dry lips across mine before he said, "My position is director of defense. It's my job to eradicate threats to Thayer."

A burst of air escaped my parted lips and I lay a hand on my heart to make sure it stayed within my chest. I was so shocked I couldn't take a full breath and sucked short, inadequate gasps of air.

My mind scattered in a dozen directions.

I tried to recall what Gresham had said to me over the course of the weeks I'd known him. I tried to process what I knew of Thayer, of Radix, of alternate forms. Why would someone as important as the Director of Thayerian Defense pursue me? Why would he become my unofficial guardian, injecting himself in my life as a mentor, a friend…a lover? What could he possibly have to gain from his association with someone like me who wasn't of this world, who didn't even know who she was?

The answer hit me like a kick to the chest. I stood heaving, trying to gain control of myself, trying not to completely fall apart. My heart physically hurt at the betrayal, and the tears that had been taunting me finally spilled over and fell hotly onto my cheeks. I bent over and held my middle, a nauseated mass.

Gresham was calling my name, but it seemed so far away. "Stella? Stella, no. No. It's not like that." He spoke almost frantically and rushed to my side.

I jerked from him, but was so off balance I had to extend my hand for support. My knees were weak and there was nothing on which to anchor, so I listed clumsily sideways before catching myself.

I closed my eyes and took several slow breaths before attempting to speak again. Nothing came. I cleared my throat, attempted to clear my mind and aimed for composure, but all I really wanted to do was crumble into a heap in the dirt.

If you'd like to be a part of the rest of Stella's journey, look for *Origin Exposed* wherever you buy books.

About the Author

Though she grew up on a working cattle ranch, it's fantasy and sci-fi that shine Jen Crane's saddle. Dragging her back to reality after reading *The Princess Bride* was a lost cause. She writes paranormal and speculative fiction novels.

Book 2 in Jen's Descended of Dragons series was selected by iTunes/iBooks as "Our Pick" in fantasy/sci-fi.

Jen has a master's degree and solid work histories in government and non-profit administration. But just in the nick of time she pronounced life *too real* for nonfiction. She now creates endearing characters and alternate realms filled with adventure, magic, and love.

Jen is happily living out her dream in The South with her husband and three children, striking that delicate balance between inspiration and frustration.

Sign up for sneak peeks, news and giveaways at
http://bit.ly/Jen_Crane_Newsletter

www.JenCraneBooks.com
Facebook: JenCraneBooks
Twitter: @JenCraneBooks
Pinterest: JenCraneBooks
Instagram: JenCraneBooks
Tumblr: JenCraneBooks

17330112R00121

Printed in Great Britain
by Amazon